It wa...
but an awful ...
through the will o...
the interior of the ...
crystals that glittere...
from the coloured pan... ...any, completely
exhausted of physical strength and drained of all
emotion, Tracy crept under the parka and hugged me to
her. And one by one the glass instruments of
the plane's control panel commenced to crack
and splinter with gunshot explosions as
the temperature fell still further . . .

By the same author

BRIAN LUMLEY

Spawn of the Winds

Grafton

An Imprint of HarperCollinsPublishers

For Gail

Grafton
An Imprint of HarperCollins*Publishers*
77–85 Fulham Palace Road,
Hammersmith, London W6 8JB

Published by Grafton 1992
9 8 7 6 5 4 3 2 1

First published by
Jove Publications, Inc., New York 1978

ISBN 0 586 21466 6

Set in Times

Printed in Great Britain by
HarperCollinsManufacturing Glasgow

Introduction

by *Professor Wingate Peaslee of Miskatonic University, Director of the Wilmarth Foundation*

In 1966 the Wilmarth Foundation recruited a telepath of exceptional talent, a man who could tune his mind to the aberrant sendings of the CCD, the Cthulhu Cycle Deities, and make a sort of sense out of what he 'heard'. Hank Silberhutte was the man: a tall, tow-headed Texan of daring and adventurous, albeit hasty and often hot-headed, inclinations.

Several years prior to his joining the Foundation, Silberhutte had lost a cousin in the cold wastes of Canada. The circumstances had been mysterious; following an unexpected cold snap of especial ferocity the party of six, engaged on government survey work, was suddenly missing, 'lost from all contact with the civilized world.' He joined in the Foundation. Having learned something of the CCD, it dawned on Silberhutte that his cousin's disappearance had coincided with strange undercurrents of unrest in the Canadian trail towns and logging camps, and with the peculiarly feverish culmination of a five-year cycle of esoteric religious festivities as practised by certain local Indians and, farther north, Eskimos.

In short, he became interested in Ithaqua, that fearful air-elemental of the CCD. It was this fascination of Silberhutte's – one might almost say obsession – which, following the very successful part he had played in a major Foundation project, prompted me to offer him the job of researching, compiling and correlating a working file or dossier on this mythical being of the Arctic snows; further, of carrying out his own survey work in Canada on the periphery of the Wind-Walker's domain, and over the line of the Arctic Circle into the interior of that frozen territory itself.

Silberhutte immediately jumped at the chance I offered and in very short order produced an almost Fortean file of related incidents and occurrences, all of them showing definite connections with that monstrous manifestation known as Ithaqua, 'the Thing that walks on the wind.' I was amazed that any single man could have accumulated so vast an amount of lore in such a short time – much of which had previously been overlooked, had gone unnoticed, or was quite frankly unknown to the Foundation archives – until I recalled that the Wind-Walker had a very special attraction for him.

Genial and affable though Hank Silberhutte invariably was, at the merest mention of elementals of the air, Eskimo legend, or cycles of morbid CCD influence, his face would harden and his eyes narrow. He was a Texan and was as proud of that fact as any man of his race, and his cousin had died in the white wastes of Ithaqua's Arctic domain. Enough said.

Perhaps in retrospect, knowing what I knew of him, I should have thought twice about giving Silberhutte the job of tracking down the Snow Thing. One needs a cool head when dealing with such horrors, and the Texan could fly off the handle in as little time as it takes to tell. But the man's physical strength and keen intelligence, his dedication and great telepathic talent, more than balanced the odds and qualified him for the tasks he might need to perform. Or so I thought.

It came about that at a time when I myself was in Denizli, directing the commencement of certain operations in Turkey, Silberhutte was making preparations for an aerial reconnaissance of the Arctic Circle, or rather of its rim, from the Bering Strait to Baffin Island. His reason for this survey, in his own words, was to allow him 'to get the feel of it; to look down on the ice-wastes from on high and see them as a great bird might see them – or as a Thing that Walks on the Wind!'

But of course there was more to his planned survey than that. There would be a strenuous series of treks to follow it, commencing before the thaws set in, for which he intended to prepare detailed routes from the air. Of these treks, one would be across the Brooks Range northwest of Fort Yukon on the Arctic Circle; another would cover a large area north of the Great Bear Lake; yet another should prove to be particularly gruelling and would take the Texan's team along the Mackenzie Mountains Trail to Aklavik.

Tough groundwork of this nature was to be a period of acclimatization for the team rather than an actual frontal attack on the Snow Thing. Those regions where Ithaqua had made his awesome presence known in the past – and where doubtless he would make it known again in the future – were to receive the team's attention at a later date, when its members had been made more able to survive by these 'toughening-up' exercises of Silberhutte's.

Finally, the third and possibly most important of all reasons for this aerial survey: he intended to put his telepathic talents to the test in a series of attempts to search out from the air the massed mental sendings of local religious cults and sects. Strangers of many lands with no easily discernible purposes were massing northward; rumours of a 'Great Coming' were legion among the barely civilized inhabitants of the whole vast region, and whispers were already filtering back to Miskatonic through strategically placed Foundation agents.

This, in the main, formed the core of my knowledge of Hank Silberhutte's initial plan of campaign against Ithaqua. Busy as I was in Denizli, he was now completely in charge of Project Wind-Walker, free to get on with it in his own way. All that I asked of him was that I be kept notified of the operation's progress.

And here I find I must insert something about Juanita Alvarez. Silberhutte was on vacation in Mexico prior to being offered Project Wind-Walker. He found Juanita in Monterrey working as an interpreter with an international firm. She was young and single, very well educated, extremely independent, she spoke four languages without a trace of accent in any of them – and she was telepathic! And here is an exceedingly strange thing; Juanita's talent was in a way as unique as Silberhutte's, for she was only telepathic with him. In exhaustive tests later carried out at Miskatonic, this proved to be an enigma that baffled all the experts. Only Hank Silberhutte could receive her mind-sendings; she in turn could only receive his. It was as if, at their first accidental meeting in Monterrey, Hank had sparked off something in her mind, something that had found and formed a unique empathy with his own extraordinary talent. They had seen one another – and they had *known*. It was as simple as that.

And of course Hank had known that this would be a major breakthrough for the Foundation, because very few members of its telepathic fraternity were actually capable of communicating with one another; those who could were usually only able to receive very vague and ill-defined mental pictures. It was not their purpose to talk telepathically with *people*, but to use their talents to detect the machinations of the lurking, alien CCD and their minions; in Hank Silberhutte and Juanita Alvarez, however, the perfect link of mental communication had been forged.

So it was to the utter despair of the theorists and telepathic technicians at Miskatonic when Hank accepted his new job, and even more so when after some months he left Arkham to travel up to Edmonton with his team, there to form a Foundation detachment for the duration of the project. In his absence they would have to temporarily suspend their attempts to discover what made Hank and Juanita tick. As Hank himself pointed out, he would not be completely out of touch; they could contact him any time they so desired – through Juanita. Still, the professors would have preferred the telepathic 'twins' together in the laboratory, in a controlled environment.

However they might have wanted it, the girl stayed on while her alter ego (that was how they had come to think of one another, even though there was absolutely nothing else between them; there was no romantic connection) was off to Canada at the start of the greatest adventure of his life. In the days that followed, try as they might, the Foundation's experts in mental telepathy could get nothing out of the girl. To all intents and purposes, except for her ability instantly to contact the Texan whenever she felt inclined or obliged to do so, she was telepathically deaf, dumb and blind.

That was how things stood when, on January 22, I received word from Miskatonic that Hank's plane was missing somewhere over the Mackenzie Mountains. Had there been an accident? A long letter from Juanita Alvarez, doubling as a report and confirming the disaster, followed. The following excerpt is part of what Hank Silberhutte's devastated alter ego had to say of the matter:

His call was like an alarm clock, waking me from nightmares that I could not quite remember – but the reality was worse than any dream. It was about 9:15 A.M. and I had slept late. Immediately I was wide awake, knowing that he had called out to me, feeling for him with my mind.

'Hank,' I answered him, speaking it out loud as well as with my mind, 'what is it?'

'Juanita!' he answered. 'Get all of this – don't miss a thing!' And then he simply opened up all his senses to me and let me see it all, everything that was happening . . .

. . . The plane was low, skimming the undersides of boiling black clouds as the pilot tried to keep his craft below the weather but above the white peaks of mountains that rushed madly by on both sides. Weaving and bucking, riding the wind wildly and whirling in mad currents of air, the plane fought its pilot like a wild animal, and through all this Hank started to tell me the story:

'We spotted him, Juanita – Ithaqua, the Wind-Walker – and our very first time out at that. It was no coincidence; we were looking for him, certainly, but he was just as surely looking for us. Or at least he was looking for me, and he certainly picked me up easily enough. We were at about N. 63°, W. 127° when we first felt it – that fantastic pull!

'. . . What a bloody fool I am, to go chasing the Snow Thing in the sky, his own element! We can forget whatever remains of that old fallacy about Ithaqua being restricted to the Arctic Circle. To the Far North, yes, but we have ample evidence that he's ventured as far south as North Manitoba, and so he could certainly –'

Abruptly he stopped consciously sending to let me see more clearly through his eyes. Only a few miles ahead of the rushing plane the white peaks reached up to the turbulent clouds. The pilot was wrestling with the controls, trying to pull the plane's nose up into the swirling cauldron above, but the wind seemed actually to be blowing now from on high, blowing *down* on the wings of the straining plane and driving it toward the harsh ice-peaks of the mountains.

Hank could see what was going to happen – what *must* happen – and now his mental transmissions became a frenzied gabble as he tried to tell me all before – before –

'We must have been somewhere between Dawson and Norman Wells when we saw him a great blot in the sky like smoke solidifying taking on a vaguely manlike but gigantic shape a beast exactly as described in the Lawton Manuscript but a description is one thing while actually to see him is –

'Then the skies darkened over in what seemed like only a few seconds and the black clouds boiled up out of nowhere and he walked up the wind on his great splayed feet and disappeared into the clouds. But before he went completely his awful face came out of the clouds to look at us through flickering carmine stars that were like the very pits of hell!

'Juanita – look!'

And again Hank's mind opened up to show me the scene he himself saw at that exact moment of time, allowing me to participate visually in his experience. It was a favour I might well have done without; the Thing that Walks on the Wind had returned.

I had read something about Ithaqua, and Hank had told me a lot more. There is one part of the legend that warns of an unholy curse; to see the Snow Thing is to be doomed, for having seen him is to know that you must become his victim – sooner or later. With me it is sooner. I can no longer close my eyes without that hideous vision of Ithaqua being there, lurking in my mind, behind my eyelids, etched on my memory's retina. Professor Peaslee, Ithaqua is a monster, indeed a 'Prime Evil', a being that never was spawned on this world and could never be accepted in any sane universe.

He – *it* – was there, perched atop that mountain peak directly ahead of the crazily lurching plane, a black bulk against the white snow and blue ice, filling the space between frozen peak and tortured sky and radiating his alienness more tangibly than the sun radiates light. To look at the sun for too long would burn one's eyes out, but to gaze into those carmine pits that Ithaqua wears for eyes – that is to scar one's very mind!

Oh, I can well believe that Ithaqua's curse might work. Out there in the snowy wastes, it must be a very strange and lonely world. A weak person, perhaps even a strong one, having seen the Wind-Walker, might easily be drawn to go in search of him, simply to prove that the nightmare he had suffered was only a nightmare. Then again, perhaps it is the being's mind that draws its victims back again, as in posthypnotic commands.

It could be so, Professor, I know it. Why, I can almost hear his command in my own mind at this very moment! But I am strong and I understand what this hellish attraction is. I can fight it.

There he was, that monster, stretching out his great arms to snatch with massive hands at the plane before it could crash into the peak, drawing it to him until the metallic grey of its wings and fuselage glowed a flickering pink and red in the reflection from the twin stars that burned in his face.

I had seen all this with Hank's own eyes, until the last moment when he deliberately shut the vision out. But even so I could still read what was in his mind. I saw the cold despair and bleak but useless anger and hatred there. So powerfully was he transmitting that I could actually feel the machine gun in my own hands as Hank put a flaming stream of tracers across the snarling dark visage of the Wind-Walker, tracers that seemed to pass right through the horror's face and into the furious clouds above.

Then Hank sought out an eye, and his shells found its centre to pour into it like a swarm of angry bees – only to burst from the back of the darkly massive head as a shower of drifting sparks! And that monstrous being threw back his head and laughed, shaking with hellish glee; but his shaking turned instantly into the hideously aberrant, spastic twitchings of indescribable madness, and this in turn gave way just as abruptly to anger and then to megalomaniac rage as finally . . . I *heard* him!

For until that last moment of time the Wind-Walker had been a creature of silence; indeed, I believe he is vocally dumb, inarticulate – but mentally . . .?

I have been told, Professor, that telepathy is telepathy and thought is thought, and there are theories and theories

12

of which the majority agree that one telepathic being sends thoughts which must be at least partially understandable to any other. It is not so. The minority which has it that truly alien thoughts would be incomprehensible are right. *Nothing* is more alien than the Wind-Walker, despite his anthropomorphism – nothing that I can imagine anyway – and his thoughts are . . . they are terrible things.

I *think* that it was an alien mixture of glee and murderous rage I heard, an obscene flux reflecting telepathically from Hank's mind like images from a cracked mirror, but the thoughts of Hank himself came to me clear as crystal in the final moment. He knew what must happen, you see, and I anticipated his shutting me out.

And I fought him because I wanted to be there, to help if I could. Oh, Hank won, but even as he drove me from his thoughts and back to my bedroom at Miskatonic, still I received impressions of the terrific acceleration he felt as Ithaqua lifted the plane high, high in his hands, even reaching up through the clouds – as a child lifts up a stone to skim across the water, or a ball to bounce.

And at the very end Hank said, *'Juanita, tell them –'*

And that was all, he was gone. There was nothing in my mind at all; it was a vacuum into which the Miskatonic morning flooded as if all the doors and windows had been opened together. And though I screamed for Hank to come back, to talk to me, all the while searching desperately for even the faintest echo of his telepathic voice, I knew that it was over.

There is one other thing, Professor. I believe that Hank's sister, Tracy Silberhutte, was on board the plane. I do not know why; she was not part of his team (in fact I do not think that she knew anything of his work with the Wilmarth Foundation), but she was certainly on board. His mind was full of her, worrying about her . . .

And Juanita was right; Tracy Silberhutte was on board Hank's plane. Later we were to discover how she came to be there, but not for a period of some four months. In the meantime Juanita, no longer of any telepathic value and having no desire to become an agent of the Wilmarth Foundation, went back to Monterrey. Search parties, both aerial and on foot, scoured the area north of Hank's last known position but found nothing; it was as if the plane had been lifted from the face of the Earth.

Then, late in May, when I was busy organizing my expedition to the Great Sandy Desert of Western Australia, Juanita returned to Miskatonic. Her arrival was as unexpected as her personal appearance was changed. She looked as though she had not had a wink of sleep in a week. She was distraught, haggard; when she saw me she threw herself into my arms and began babbling hysterically and incoherently. Plainly she had received a terrific shock.

I immediately ordered that a sedative be administered and that she be put to bed. Even under sedation, however, she rambled on about Hank, about his being alive somewhere, and about the terrible winds that blow between the worlds and the thing that walks those winds, often carrying its victims with it out of this place and time into alien voids.

When the effects of the sedative wore off, experts at the University verified that she was indeed in contact with someone; but while they were able to detect the phenomenon of telepathic communication, they were completely at a loss as to whom *exactly* she was talking to. There was only one thing to do and that was to accept what she said as truth.

It was at this point, too, that one of my 'hunchmen' – a member of a team of psychically aware specialists, the scientifically enlightened counterparts of medieval mediums and spiritualists – asked me a rather strange question. Quite casually, he stopped me to ask if Hank Silberhutte had ever been an astronaut.

I might normally have laughed but was in no mood. Instead I told him curtly that no, Silberhutte had never been an astronaut – what was this, some sort of macabre riddle? He answered in these words, which I will always remember:

'No riddle, Professor, and no offence intended – but after all I am a hunchman. And I'll tell you something: I'd bet a month's salary that it *is* Hank Silberhutte who's trying to contact Miss Alvarez. And one other thing – wherever he's transmitting from, it's no part of this Earth!'

On the morning of June 3 Juanita began picking up a very clear telepathic transmission. The following narrative, relayed through her mind from incredible and unknown voids of space and time, was recorded exactly as she received it.

Part One

1

Winds of the Void

(Recorded through the Medium of Juanita Alvarez)

I'm sorry about that, Juanita. I realize now that it must have given you a terrific jolt to receive what must have seemed like messages from a dead man. But I've been trying to reach you ever since we got here three months ago, and –

You say it's been *four* months? Well, that tells me something; it took us a month to get here. And during that month we were all dead to the world except for Tracy, who had the stone, and of course poor Dick Selway, the pilot. He was just . . . dead. I'm not being callous, Juanita, but it's been three pretty hellish months for us, one way or another, and we've seen enough of death in that time to –

We? Yes, Tracy, Jimmy Franklin, Paul White and myself. All right, I'll go right back to square one for you, Juanita – back to where I cut you off when I thought that Ithaqua was going to flatten the plane against that mountain . . .

Oh, I knew we were done for, no doubt about it. And that damned . . . *Thing*! He was massive enough when we first spotted him – shapeless, writhing like disturbed smoke, big as a building – but when he has a mind to he can simply, well, *expand*. He was just starting to puff himself up when he caught hold of the plane with a hand black as night, five-fingered but like a bird's claw, with talons instead of fingers, and his strength was unbelievable.

I thought he intended to crush us; I actually saw the inner wall of the fuselage starting to buckle as he tightened his grip. But then he lifted us up into the sky, way up above those clouds, and for an instant he paused in that position. Juanita, I admit that when he did that I just closed my eyes, gritted my teeth and prayed. And I'm not a man that prays too often.

That was when Tracy grabbed me. Scared to death, all tears and snuffles, just like when she was a little kid sister. She threw her arms around my neck, and I felt the star-stone pressed between us.

I hadn't realized it but the thing outside the plane must have been listening and watching inside my head. He pounced on the picture of that star-stone right there in my mind, stared for a split second – then threw it straight back, withdrawing his mind from mine completely. Only after he had gone was I sure he'd ever been there.

Now, I suppose you caught his thoughts when he was – laughing? – just before he grabbed the plane? Well, I've since learned that his mind-talk can only be picked up when he's really angry or, yes, frightened. Even then, though, his thoughts can't positively be interpreted. But still I somehow knew that when the great beast saw the star-stone in my mind it had shocked him rigid, frightened him. And it had made him angry!

He was snarling and mewling in a frenzy of frustration and rage. I guessed right away then that he couldn't hurt us, not directly at any rate, and for the first time since I joined the Foundation I really appreciated the power of the five-pointed stars. Think of it – a thing that can walk on the wind, an alien monster from God only knows what infinities of space and time – and a little star-shaped stone from Miskatonic's kilns rendered him powerless to harm us. Almost.

No, he couldn't directly hurt us any worse than he had already, but he certainly didn't intend to let us off lightly.

By then I think Dick Selway was already dead. He'd cracked his head against the control panel and there was blood everywhere; he just hung limp, trapped in the pilot's seat. Still, even with Dick gone, if Ithaqua had let go of the plane right then – which I thought he was going to for a second – I think that perhaps I could have landed her. And I believe the horror outside picked *that* little fact right out of my head, too. Only he had worked it out differently.

After being hoisted up to the sky, I had fallen back away from the gun in the nose; now Paul White, hunchman and photographer, made it up there hand over hand and checked Dick Selway's pulse. Whitey cursed softly and pushed Dick's body over to one side, then wedged himself against the gun. He had taken all the pictures he wanted; now he wanted something else.

Jimmy Franklin was still on the radio but getting nowhere; the aerial must have been ripped away. And so Whitey started hammering away with the tracers, hitting the Wind-Walker almost point-blank right in those eyes of his. And all he got for his pains was a shower of harmless sparks from somewhere at the back of Ithaqua's head.

Then the creature was off with us, loping across the Arctic skies in lengthening strides that took us even farther north and farther – *up*! The ice-wastes fell away beneath the plane as we rose into the sky ever faster; the acceleration was tremendous and I was slammed against the buckled wall of the fuselage with Tracy still in my arms.

Whitey, shaken loose from the gun, whirled by us and fell down into the tail section as the whole plane suddenly tilted. Before I blacked out I managed to clear the frost from one of the windows. Looking out I saw a black sky, and away and below I could plainly make out the curve of the Earth.

Yes, frost on the windows, Juanita. That started the moment Ithaqua grabbed us; ice formed on the inside as well as the outside of the plane, but without making us feel any normal sort of chill. Oh, yes, it was a strange cold.

Not merely the subzero temperatures of Arctic climes but an iciness unique in Ithaqua and the weird ways he treads. It was the bitter chill of the winds that blow between the worlds.

From then on until we touched down on the littered plains of Borea – beneath vast, pitted triplet moons that hung low over the plateau on the horizon, eternally frozen in a starless sky – Whitey, Jimmy and I were unconscious. Yes, for a whole month, it seems. Some sort of deep-frozen suspended animation, I suppose. But not Tracy.

Oh, she passed out initially, but later she regained consciousness while we were still en route. She didn't know that right off, though, for there was no sensation of movement or acceleration. She believed that we were down somewhere in the mountains; coming from outside was an eerie whine or hum, like the thin winds of high peaks. The inside of the plane was all white with frost; the windows were completely iced over and opaque; she could detect no sign of life in any of us and our bodies were heavily rimed with frost. Poor kid, she could hardly be blamed for thinking that we were all dead.

Yet in a way she was lucky, too, because the door of the plane was frozen shut, and though she put everything she could into getting it open it simply wouldn't budge. God knows what might have happened if she *had* opened that door!

It was when she realized that she couldn't get out of the plane that Tracy panicked and tried to smash one of the windows in the nose. Well, she could make no impression on the window either, but she did manage to clear the frost and ice away from an area of the glass. And so she looked out.

Picture it for yourself, Juanita: to be in a plane full of icy corpses, like the interior of some weirdo outsize freezer, listening to a strange rushing hum, like a distant wind blowing through a thousand telegraph wires. To know the nightmare of being lost and alone, trapped in an ice-tomb high in mountain fastnesses. And then to peep out and discover that as bad as your plight might have seemed a moment ago, its terrors could never have equalled the horror facing you now. For staring right back at her, with the plane held at arm's length in front of him as he flew through the star-voids, was Ithaqua, the Thing that Walks on the Wind!

Strange starlanes – a hyperspace dimension where inconceivable currents rush and roar in interstellar spaces – and a being of utterly alien energies who knows the ways between the spheres as an eel knows the derelict and weed-strewn deeps of the dark Sargasso. But it wasn't only this sudden inundating flood of revelation that caused Tracy to faint away on the frosted floor of the plane. Neither that nor the sight of strange stars shooting dizzyingly by – like summer showers of meteorites magnified a thousand times – as Ithaqua hurtled through the void. No, it was the *look* on the Wind-Walker's face. It was those eyes, seeming to peel away the metal hull of the plane like tinsel to stare into Tracy's very soul. For she knew that those eyes saw her even as they narrowed in that inhuman face – and she knew, too, that they had filled suddenly with all the lusts of hell.

Thinking back to what Tracy told me when I came out of the freeze on Borea, I'm inclined to believe that time must be different for Ithaqua when he glides along the star winds, and for anything he carries with him. Not slowed down, as might be expected, but accelerated somehow. According to our calculations we've been on Borea for three months, and we left Earth four months ago, but Tracy reckons she slept only three or four times during the whole trip. As for myself, I wouldn't know one way or the other. I do remember dreams – of Tracy's head on my cold chest and her hands on my face, and her voice, crying out to me about the horror outside the plane.

But that's jumping things a bit. I'll tell it as Tracy told it to me.

When she came to after her faint it was dark; she'd accidentally knocked off the cabin lights when she slipped down the wall. The control-panel lights were still on though, and she could see well enough in their glow. Deciding to leave the main lights off to conserve the batteries, she set about making herself a sandwich and some coffee.

That was when she first noticed that despite the ice and frost everywhere she herself was not unbearably cold. And the star-stone about her neck was warm.

She felt a lot better after a bite to eat and a cup of hot coffee; but she kept well away from the windows and refused even to think about what was outside. And through all this there was no sensation of free-falling, none of the physiological phenomena of spaceflight at all; which leads me to believe that in fact Ithaqua was moving *between* dimensions.

Then Tracy noticed another queer thing. She had moved over to sit beside me on the cabin floor, and as she sipped the last of her coffee she saw that my right arm had moved; it had left a clear space in the frost on the rubberized surface of the deck. She caught her breath. I couldn't be alive, could I? No, not possibly. There I was, white as a snowflake and looking stiff as mutton in a freezer. But putting her ear to my chest Tracy listened breathlessly until she heard a heartbeat. Just one, and then several seconds later, another.

From then on, except during those periods when she was sleeping, Tracy spent her time frantically trying to rouse me from my strange, frozen sleep; not only me but Whitey and Jimmy, too. Jimmy Franklin lost the skin off his lower lip through Tracy's ministrations with hot coffee! But for all this she was out of luck and had to be satisfied with the knowledge that at least we were alive when by rights we ought to have been dead.

The answer, of course, lay in the star-stones of ancient Mnar, but she didn't know that. Besides the stone she wore about her neck there was one other aboard the plane – in the first-aid cabinet, of all places. That was Paul White's stone. If it weren't for those stones we really would have been dead by then, all of us. Only their presence in the plane had forced the Wind-Walker to exercise restraint. The ancient magic of the Elder Gods was still at work.

Like myself, this was for Whitey his first really active stint with the Wilmarth Foundation, and he had made the same mistake as I had. I had always sort of scorned the star-stones, in the way a greenhorn soldier might scorn a bulletproof vest before he's seen the terrible mess a bullet can make of a man's chest – or in my case, before I really knew the kind of horror a Thing that Walks on the Wind might wreak. Whitey, a do-it-by-the-book man, had brought his stone along all right but felt stupid wearing it, so he'd placed it in the plane's first-aid cabinet out of the way. Dick Selway and Jimmy Franklin, greener in the ways of the CCD even than Whitey and I, hadn't bothered with their stones at all! And all Tracy knew of these things, of the star-stones, was that the one she wore about her neck, which by then she'd forgotten was there at all, had been my good luck charm, my rabbit's foot.

In fact that star-stone was Tracy's reason for being on the plane in the first place. It was pure coincidence that she had been staying with friends in Edmonton for a few days while I was starting out on Project Wind-Walker. The night before we started the flying programme I attended a party at the home of her friends. I had a few drinks and must have mentioned something of my preparatory work at the airfield. The next morning when Paul White picked me up, I forgot my star-stone and left it in the room where

I had bunked down. Tracy found it. Since she intended to start the long trip back down to our home in Texas that same morning, she decided to go via the airfield and return the stone to me. Driving out to the field, she worked out a little prank to play on me.

For some time Tracy and my father had been speculating on my work with 'The Government', and now finally her curiosity had gotten the better of her. She saw this situation as a chance to find out what it was all about.

The Foundation had secured for my team an outlying area of the airport; a fenced-off, run-down, dusty area with its own rather worse-for-wear landing strip. But it was good enough for us and anyway, our plane was no luxury airliner. We had also been supplied with a full-time guard for the gated entrance, though I have to admit that I didn't brief him well. I was hardly expecting trouble, certainly not Tracy's sort. She arrived at the gates, told the guard who she was and showed him my star-stone. She said I had forgotten it and she knew I wouldn't want to go off without it.

Well, Tracy's a damned good-looking girl. She probably turned on the charm. And since the guard could have no idea just what she intended to do, I don't suppose he could really be blamed for letting her in. . . .

Delighted with herself that her plan was working out, Tracy parked her car behind a hangar and sneaked over to our plane. She couldn't mistake it. It was the only one, standing out on the runway close to the hangar. The door was open; she climbed in and tucked herself away in the tail, and that was that.

Some time later, together with the three legitimate members of my team, I left our headquarters shack at the other side of the field and slung my gear into our jeep. We drove to the plane and boarded. Tracy didn't show herself until we were airborne and well to the north. And like a fool, after first blowing my stack, I decided to let her stay. To head back then would have been to slow the work down for a whole day, and the team was anxious to get on with the job. In any case, there wouldn't be a great deal for Tracy to see, would there?

So that was how she came to be on board, and looking back now I suppose it's just as well for the rest of us that she was. God only knows what our fate might have been without her. But I've been straying a bit, I think.

After her third or fourth period of sleep, Tracy woke to an unsettling, irritable and unaccustomed feeling quite different from any emotional disturbance she might have expected to suffer in her present circumstances. She felt drawn somehow to the frosted windows, and even began to clear a large area of one of them before she realized what she was doing, but not before the huge form of the horror hurtling through the void outside began to take on an ominous shape through the glass.

Then Tracy knew that the compulsion she felt and the inner voice she heard in her head insistently demanding that she warm the glass of the window until it cleared to its normal transparency, was not her own but the hypnotically telepathic voice of the being who now rushed with the plane on an unguessable course. And recognizing the fact that she knew him, Ithaqua grew angry. He doubled, then redoubled his mental effort to control her.

She saw his alien lust clearly in her mind even as she stepped closer to the window, reaching out her warm, trembling zombie hands to the task imposed by the Wind-Walker's will. And she knew too, his purpose; to bend her mind, body and soul, completely and everlastingly to his will through those evilly flaring eyes of his, which loomed dully behind an all-too-thin layer of frosted glass.

And instinctively, impelled by horror alone, Tracy's hands flew to her breast, finding my star-shaped talisman there and unconsciously pressing that sigil of the Elder Gods to her heart. Instantly the Wind-Walker withdrew from her mind, recoiling and shrivelling before that abhorred symbol of the power of Good as a feather before a candle's flame. And Tracy did not know why, suddenly, the magnet pull on her mind was at an end, leaving her stumbling, numb, almost completely drained of strength. She only knew that beyond the semi-opaque window those eyes blazed more hideously yet, and that the plane now shook like a toy in the fist of a demented giant as Ithaqua's rage brought on a massive trembling.

She moved away from the window on unsteady legs and gradually the shaking of the plane subsided. For a spell she moved dazedly about the aircraft, listening to the maddeningly slow beatings of our hearts and doing what she could to improve our comfort until, feeling hunger stir, she turned herself again to making coffee and preparing something to eat. And as she was about that task, the temperature began to drop in the aircraft, plunging in the space of only a minute or so from its previously frozen chill into sub-zero temperatures. A sheet of deep white stretched itself over the windows of the nose and fuselage, completely obscuring once more the horror sailing on the winds of the void outside. Icy fingers spread over the metal walls, rubber floor coverings, equipment and motionless men.

It was no natural cold, but an awful condition brought about through the will of Ithaqua. As such it could not affect Tracy, unknowingly protected as she was by the star-shaped symbol of Eld that she wore about her neck; instead it speeded her to the task of throwing extra blankets over our all but inanimate forms where they lay about the floor, to insulate us as much as possible from the incredible cold.

Having done what she could for us and astonished and frightened that she herself should feel nothing of the effects of the plummeting temperature, Tracy turned once more to her coffee, only to discover that though the electricity still freely flowed, nevertheless the water had frozen solid in the kettle. Only then, briefly, did she think of giving in, bursting into tears and crying unashamedly as she tried once more, futilely, to shake me awake.

The depth of frost thickened in the interior of the plane, blanketing it in white crystals that glittered in the glow from coloured panel lights. Finally, completely exhausted of physical strength and drained of emotion, Tracy lay down beside me and crept under the parka that covered me, hugging my cold form to her. And one by one the glass instruments of the pilot's control panel cracked and splintered as the temperature fell still lower.

2

World of the Winds

(Recorded through the Medium of Juanita Alvarez)

When Tracy next awakened it was to find her body a mass of bruises and aching bones. The interior of the plane was in complete disorder but – miracle of miracles! – her three 'corpses' were all stirring, and we were groaning almost with one voice. I can vouch for that last. I most certainly was groaning! My entire body felt swollen and inflamed.

We had obviously been tossed down hard. The door was hanging open on snapped safety bolts; one of the windows had been shattered outward, I guessed by a box of ammunition flying against it; the broken box and a number of ammunition belts were strewn across the narrow deck. Snow was hissing softly in through the open door and broken window, settling in small drifts on the tilted floor. The nose of the plane was down, tail up, at an angle of between fifteen and twenty degrees. I remember thinking as I climbed stiffly, painfully to my feet that I ought to feel terribly cold, so high up in the mountains of the far North. . . .

Then it was a matter of fighting Tracy off. She was hysterical with relief, going from me to Whitey, then to Jimmy, finally back to me, crying and kissing us and babbling out her story, which I gradually began to take in. It took me a few moments to get oriented. I seemed to be more or less whole – nothing broken at any rate, despite the multiple aches and pains – and Whitey seemed fine, too, just a little shaken up. But Jimmy had a nasty bump on his head and he hadn't quite managed to get to his feet yet.

Since it was plain we weren't about to die or stiffen up on her again, Tracy soon calmed down enough to make coffee. She was shivering like a leaf in a gale, which I believed was probably just as much the result of shaken nerves as physical coldness. I managed to get the door shut and fixed up a blanket over the broken window. That would keep some of the cold out, at least. Even though I didn't feel any real discomfort myself, there was no telling what shock might do to the others. One glance out of the door as I closed it had been sufficient to confirm at least part of Tracy's story; we certainly weren't down in any mountains. Outside, under lowering clouds, a vast white plain stretched away, with strangely shaped hummocks of snow dotting it at intervals. In the distance I could just make out what looked like – but then the snow blew up like an opaque white curtain. It was a relief, though, to note that if Tracy's story should prove to be one hundred per cent fact and not fifty per cent fancy, fever or nightmare, then at least there was no sign of the Wind-Walker for the moment. Wherever he had gone, I hoped he would stay there.

But why wasn't I cold? Already the blanket at the open window had frozen stiff as a board, and Tracy was still shivering as if she would shake herself to pieces. I noticed that like myself, Whitey and Jimmy didn't seem uncomfortable, and immediately something began tugging at the back of my memory, something I had read of Ithaqua. The Wind-Walker was able to bring about alterations in the body temperatures of those he contaminated. Were we then contaminated? I suspected that my sister was not.

Breaking into my thoughts, Tracy passed me a steaming cup of coffee. Her hands were white and they shook. I looked at the cup for a moment, then passed it right back. 'You drink it, Tracy. I think you need it more than I do.'

I shrugged out of my outsize parka and wrapped it around her shoulders over the one she wore already, zipping it up the front. Then I moved past Jimmy, on his feet now, and opened up the first aid cabinet. The kit inside was all tumbled about but I found a clinical thermometer and put

31

it under my tongue. I also found Whitey's star-stone.

I lifted the thing out of the debris of bandages and bottles, turning to the other three. 'Who does this belong –' I started to mumble around the thermometer – then dropped the star-stone. It was hot as hell! A tiny puff of steam or smoke rose up from my stinging fingers; the skin of my palm was cracked where I had held the five-pointed star.

'That's mine,' Whitey said, sipping his coffee and starting to look a lot more human. He was frowning, plainly wondering why I had dropped the star-stone. 'What's up?'

Tracy hurried over and took hold of my damaged hand, staring in astonishment at the redly blistering flesh, then at me, finally stooping to pick up the star-stone. I started to stop her until I saw that she plainly couldn't feel the thing's heat. But was it really hot?

I took the thermometer out of my mouth and squinted at it. The scale started at 35° Centigrade, its lowest point – useful if someone were suffering from extreme hypothermia or exposure – but the mercury wasn't showing at that level. It had shrunk back into a silver blob at the frozen end of the scale. I was dead, or should be!

I knew then that Whitey and Jimmy would be the same. Wherever we were, well it could get as cold as it damn well wanted to; *we* weren't going to freeze to death. But Tracy was something else again.

Obviously the star-stone she wore had saved her from this effect of close proximity to the Wind-Walker, but it had also left her as vulnerable to normal low temperatures as she had been before, as any normal person always is. Now I could see why Ithaqua had placed this weird stricture upon us, why Whitey, Jimmy and I had suffered this incredible change. This way Ithaqua wouldn't have to worry about our threatening him with our star-stones. We wouldn't be able to touch the damned things.

I looked at the others and saw a little of the panic hidden in their eyes, the grim fears hiding behind the white masks

32

of their faces. The telepathic impressions I was getting were nervous, disorganized, bordering on the hysterical. Things needed sorting out right now, before matters got worse.

'Tracy,' I said, 'you'd better put that second stone around your neck along with the other. We can hardly afford to lose them, and you're the only one who can handle them.' I brought out my metal security box from where it was stowed beneath a seat and unlocked it, taking out a duplicate copy of my complete file on Project Wind-Walker.

'You'd better read this, too,' I said, passing her the heavy file of papers and documents. 'Then you'll know what you've gotten yourself into.'

While I was busy dealing with Tracy's education, Whitey took a small electric heater from among the items in his personal kit, a tiny Japanese model with its own adapter. He plugged it into a battery-fed outlet. In a matter of only a minute or so warm air began to pour from the grill, driven by a hidden fan. Whitey directed the stream of warmth at Tracy where she sat turning the pages of my file and sipping her coffee.

'All right,' I said to the two men, inclining my head toward the back of the fuselage. We moved into a rather cramped huddle.

'Boys,' I started, 'I think we're in a pretty bad mess, and I admit that I'm mainly to blame. Things happened a lot too fast for me; but that's no excuse, or at best a lame one. Up to now this has been a pretty messed-up job. And again, well, I suppose the fault is mine; I *know* it's mine. So if you're starting to feel that it's high time we voted in a new chief, then –'

'You're joking, Hank!' Whitey's naturally mournful voice cut me off in mid-sentence, his eyebrows seeming to droop from the centre where they met over his nose as he frowned.

'No way,' Jimmy agreed with Whitey, shaking his head, dark eyes bright in his bronze face. 'You got us into this, you get us out.'

33

They were both smiling now, albeit lopsidedly. Whitey continued, 'I'm a hunchman, Hank, and it's my bet that you'll boss this show no matter what anyone else decides. Anyway, we're all equally to blame for what's happened.'

'All right,' I told them, relieved that they were still with me, 'but that's something else we need to decide; just exactly what *has* happened. I don't know if you were listening to Tracy while she was going on about all she saw, her experiences since the Big Fellow grabbed us?'

'I was listening,' Whitey answered, his eyebrows drooping again.

Jimmy nodded grimly. 'Sounded to me like Tracy believes we're no longer on Earth.'

'Yes, that's what it sounded like,' I agreed. 'But we'll talk about that in a minute. First I want to clear up this thing with the star-stones.'

'Confession,' Jimmy sheepishly offered. 'I forgot to bring mine.'

'I wouldn't feel too bad about it,' I told him. 'I forgot mine, too. If it weren't for Tracy we'd only have the one – Whitey's. And I have a feeling that we didn't simply "forget" them, either. No, it wasn't bravado but something else. The Wind-Walker is telepathic; if anyone knows that I do. If I'm right, then it's an even bet he's known about us all along, probably right from the moment Peaslee decided we should have a go at him. I think he's been applying subtle telepathic pressures that have gone completely undetected. I can show you evidence for what I say. Here's Whitey, a strong-willed man. He brings along his stone but then doesn't wear it. Then I conveniently "forget" my stone. You, Jimmy, and poor Dick – you don't bother with your stones at all! Oh, yes, I guess we can be truly thankful for Tracy. She's thrown one hell of a monkeywrench right in Ithaqua's works.'

'And my star-stone really burned you?' Whitey asked, confirming more than questioning the fact.

'Would you like to go and ask Tracy to let you have it back?' I said. 'Perhaps wear it round your neck?' I showed him my blistered hand.

'I'll take your word for it. But how?'

Here Jimmy cut in. 'I think I know. When Ithaqua grabbed the plane we were unprotected, all of us except Tracy. I must have read everything you ever put together, Hank, on Ithaqua. Don't know of a single case where he was involved when there wasn't some mention of this tremendous drop in body temperature. He – he *changes* people!'

'Right,' I put in. 'He brings them under his influence, subtly alters them, imbues them, I believe, with something of his own aura, which he radiates as intense cold.'

Jimmy chewed his lip. 'Isn't that a whole lot of guesswork, Hank?'

'Not really,' I answered. 'The star-stone burned me, didn't it? Just like I was Ithaqua myself, or one of his minions.'

'Are you saying that we are – his?'

'Not necessarily. You've read the case histories. There was that woman, Lucille Bridgeman. She certainly didn't knuckle under to him, and she suffered the same fate. In fact I think we may soon be glad we're immune to the cold. Wherever we are, it seems a pretty grim place. *We* should be all right, but we'll have to look after Tracy. She's more than just my sister; she's the only one who can handle the star-stones. As long as she can do that we're "untouchable" – I hope.'

'Maybe,' Whitey interrupted, 'maybe we *have* to be immune to the cold simply to live here.'

'I know what you mean. You think that Ithaqua has acclimatized us, right?'

'Something like that, yes,' he answered.

'Which brings us back to an earlier question,' Jimmy put in. 'Just where *is* this place? Where the hell are we?'

'That's something that will have to wait, for now,' I told him. 'There are other things we have to do. We ought to take inventory, see what we've got that we can use, decide what should be done immediately, and work out plans to cover as many eventualities as we can think of. That last should be a good one for you, Whitey, although at the moment it's the least important of the lot. Survival is the main thing, but we don't know until the snow clears just exactly what our position is. Or how to improve it.'

'Obviously we can't stay in the plane,' Jimmy said. 'Not for any great length of time. But if we are going to move on, we'll need to take as much of our kit with us as we can carry.'

'The door will lift right off its hinges,' Whitey said. 'It ought to make a good sledge.'

'And of course we have our guns,' Jimmy butted in. 'There's a rifle in Dick's kit, and a couple of pistols. He was looking after the weapons side of it, but now –' He let it tail off, his eyes straying to the nose of the plane where a frozen shape lay wrapped in blankets.

'Yes,' I nodded, 'and we'll need to take care of Dick, too.'

Whitey added, 'If we're going to leave the plane anyway, I think perhaps Dick would be just as happy if he stayed right here. Captain of his ship, so to speak.'

I nodded. 'Maybe you're right. Right now I suggest we see what we can pack away. We'll carry the weapons openly, of course. Jimmy, you can start –'

'Hank!' Tracy suddenly shouted, her voice somehow managing to rise hysterically in the space of that single exclamation.

I half-leaped, half-skidded down the frosted floor of the tilted fuselage to where she stood at a window. She had cleared the frost from one corner of the glass. Outside the snow had stopped. The great plain with its strange snow hummocks stood out stark against a dull grey sky. In the

36

distance a pyramidal structure stood up from the snow. At its apex – a shape. And that shape was unmistakable.

'Ithaqua!' I heard myself say, the name hissing off my tongue.

The two men joined me as Tracy moved shakily away from the window, her hand to her throat. Clearing the frost from a larger area of the glass, I asked, 'How far, do you think?'

'Mile and a half, two miles,' Jimmy answered, producing a pair of binoculars. He put them to his eyes. 'God, look at that – *horror*!'

I took the binoculars from him, put them to my eyes, and the distant scene sprang up large as life. Indeed, the Wind-Walker was larger than life; a fantastic, towering shape, black as a starless night, with gaping eyes that glowered and burned in his awful face. He straddled the apex of the pyramid on massive legs, gesticulating with his threatening arms.

Gesticulating, threatening what? Whom?

I increased the magnification of the binoculars and followed the outline of the pyramid down to its base. People, a crowd of them, on their knees, heads down in supplication – worshippers.

Their faces were indistinct, blurred, but I could see that they were a squat, dark people, most of them. Of Eskimo or Mongol origins, perhaps.

At the front of this prone assembly stood two men, whites, long-haired and dressed in black robes. Priests or spokesmen. Managing to get the magnification just right at last, I focused upon the nearer of the two. European, at a guess; his gaunt face seemed full of fanatic fervour. I turned my attention to the pyramid, Ithaqua's 'altar'. I judged the thing to be all of eighty, maybe ninety feet in height.

'That pyramid is like a damned junk-pile!' I gasped. 'A heap of scrap sheathed in ice. Near the base there's what looks like a small airplane. Yes, I can see the cockpit clearly, and part of one wing. Halfway up there's some sort of tracked vehicle, and a bit higher something that looks like the gondola of a balloon. And, by God, I believe there's a heavy-duty truck in there as well! Other stuff, too, things I can't quite identify. All encased in ice, frozen solid.'

I went on to describe the worshippers at the base of the conglomerate cone, then did a slow sweep of the plain in its immediate vicinity. 'There are totems. Huge carved totems circling the pyramid; Eskimo, I'm sure of it, and crowned with effigies of Ithaqua. These are his worshippers, all right, and this is their place of worship.'

I looked again at the thing standing splay-footed atop its altar, with one great misshapen foot resting upon what looked like the jutting bonnet of an automobile, the other gripping a second projection on the opposite side of the ice pyramid. As I did so I saw him fling out an arm in my direction, the hand pointing.

His black face with its alien contours and flaring eyes convulsed briefly, then turned to stare in the direction of the pointing hand, towards the plane. His other hand lifted high to the leaden sky and the great fist clenched. He struck himself in the chest with a downward-sweeping, imperious blow.

By that time Whitey had found a second pair of binoculars. He too had seen these last actions of the Wind-Walker. 'He's giving orders,' Whitey said. 'Can you get to him telepathically, Hank?'

'I daren't,' I answered. 'Not right now. For the moment he holds all the aces. Later, if the situation improves – then, maybe –'

'In that case I'll voice a hunch; a pretty safe one, too, I think.'

'Let me take a guess at it,' I said, thinking about what I had just seen. 'You think we've been sent for – that Ithaqua has told his boys to come and get us, right?'

Whitey frowned, his eyebrows drooping ominously. He handed his binoculars to Jimmy, then looked around to make sure Tracy was out of the way. She had moved up close to the tiny heater and had her nose stuck deep in my file again, seemingly absorbed in it. 'Not necessarily *us*,' Whitey quietly corrected me. 'I don't think Ithaqua gives a hoot for us.' He grimaced. 'Except perhaps for our entertainment value. But,' he nodded in Tracy's direction, 'your sister –'

At that same moment she looked up, meeting our gaze. She had been listening in on us after all. 'I've just been reading all about him,' she said, her face ashen. 'About his appetites. You don't need to whisper.'

'Forget it, Tracy,' I told her, anger roughening my voice. 'No harm will come to you. I'll see to that, no matter what.'

She tried to smile, failed to make it all the way and settled for a tragicomic pose with her hands held up before her against an unseen menace. 'A fate worse than death!' she shrilled, much too shrilly.

'You just hang onto those star-stones, Tracy,' Jimmy Franklin told her from the nose of the plane. He had taken the gun off its mountings and now dragged it into position in front of the closed door. 'Old Windy will hardly dare to bother you while you have those hanging round your neck.' He sat behind the gun and traversed it left to right and back again on its swivel, squinting down the sights. 'Just let us worry about the rest of it, all right?'

3

Children of the Winds

(Recorded through the Medium of Juanita Alvarez)

From that time on our salvage work went ahead full speed, with one brief break when Tracy called us over to look out of a window she had cleared of frost on that side of the plane away from the altar of the Snow-Thing. And if we had needed convincing that indeed we were stranded on a world other than our own Earth, now we were convinced.

Tracy had started on the job of clearing the windows when she saw how quickly the steady increase in temperature in the plane was breaking up the ice and frost. Obviously we were now subject to a 'natural' cold as opposed to the preternatural iciness generated by the Wind-Walker. The plane's batteries were quickly failing, true, but Whitey's heater had sent the temperature in the plane soaring, however temporarily. That the frost inside the aircraft and the ice on its wings and fuselage were formed initially through the presence of Ithaqua seemed undeniable, but obviously in the Wind-Walker's absence the frozen inorganic residuum of his passing became subject once more to mundane laws and conditions.

Unfortunately the same was not true for my crew. Tracy appreciated the warmth, of course. That was obvious from the way she had thrown off ·her parkas. We three men, however, remained in that same cold condition to which we had awakened. Not that we *felt* physically cold in ourselves; no, though our body temperatures were such as would not normally support human life, we suffered no abnormal discomfort whatever. To further complicate matters our circulatory and respiratory systems, in fact almost the entire scale of our physiological functions, seemed somehow contracted, slowed down. But not, mercifully, the speed of our mental and physical reactions and responses.

A very ironic situation to say the least: Tracy was affected quite normally by low temperatures of natural sources, but protected from the monstrous machineries of the Wind-Walker while the rest of us were impervious to subzero temperatures but incapable of handling the only real weapons we had against our awesome enemy.

But there I go, straying from the point again.

Let me show you the scene as we viewed it once the windows of our aircraft were back to their normal state of transparency. To one side of us, sloping almost imperceptibly down and away from our crippled machine, stretched a great white expanse that reached to a distant and grey horizon, an expanse dotted here and there with strange piles of snow whose often fascinatingly familiar shapes kept drawing my eyes to them more and more frequently as time passed.

To the other side, topping a very gradually rising slope, a vast, sheer-sided hump of rock sat at a distance of some four to five miles. This solitary feature in the otherwise featureless white expanse was a relief to the eyes, though I admit we speculated rather morbidly about the black tunnel entrances that could be seen in the base of the massive, plateau-like formation. There was life there too, showing especially in an increasing amount of activity about the mouths of the tunnels and behind turrets cut into the icy roof of the ominous stone face, but our binoculars were not strong enough to show just who or what was responsible for this activity, or to what end it was directed.

And how did all of this tell us that we were no longer on Mother Earth? Couldn't we have been somewhere in Canada, in Greenland or Baffin Island, or maybe even Siberia? Well, perhaps we could have been – but not with

41

those three great moons hanging in the sky behind the plateau!

All grey and green, those moons, completely awe-inspiring in the grandeur they lent the otherwise desolate scene. These were the Moons of Borea, though we were not to know what this place was called until later; and those moons moved across the heavens not at all but hung immobile and unchanging always over the horizon. Even the most distant of the three orbs, its disc three-quarters hidden by that of the second, was bigger than the moon of Earth as we had known it.

And it was as I stood there in awe of this scene that Tracy, whose fearful interest was firmly and not surprisingly centred in Ithaqua rather than in this alien planet and its moons, called out to me from the other side of the plane. Two short strides took me to her side; Jimmy and Whitey crowded a second window.

For the better part of an hour while we had worked in the plane the Wind-Walker had simply stood, arms folded across his chest, atop the distant pyramid. His worshippers had remained kneeling during that period, while their lord and master stared out through partly lidded eyes over their heads and across the white plains. Now, however, he was expanding, raising his arms up to the skies, growing upward and outward faster and faster until, billowing skyward like some djinn from an Arabian bottle, he bent his legs and thrust himself up.

Then his great webbed feet spread wide and he walked the wind that suddenly came rushing out of nowhere. Rising up and up, he turned, headed towards the Moons of Borea and, passing high over our plane in an instant, finally seemed to dwindle to a dot and vanish over the distant horizon. Only once did he pause; that was when he passed over the plateau. Then his gravity-defying

42

steps seemed to falter momentarily and his great head inclined toward the world below. His eyes turned almost sulphurous as he gazed intently down; his great arms seemed to reach toward the plateau, about which no single sign of life could now be seen. But then he checked himself and was off again, striding into the heavens. From the time he left his position atop the pyramid, he passed completely out of sight in less than twenty seconds.

That strange wind the Snow-Thing had called up carried now to the plane, flurrying the loose snow in white wind-devils and bringing with it the cries and ululations of Ithaqua's worshippers as they voiced their songs of praise. Eerily they reached out to us on the lessening squalls that shook the frozen blanket where I had fastened it up, filling the plane with an ominous foreboding.

'Batteries are nearly dead,' Whitey said, cocking an ear at the dying whir of the heater.

'Yes, I think it's pretty near time we were leaving,' I told him. 'Tracy, you'd better get back into your parka. Wrap yourself up as much as you can.'

Standing at the window as before, with a pair of binoculars lifted to her eyes, she answered, 'His worshippers are leaving the altar. They – they seem to be – disappearing!'

Again I moved to her side, taking the binoculars from her. For half a minute I gazed. 'They're leaving, yes, but not disappearing. They have white cloaks or pelts; when they use them to cover their bodies they seem to vanish against the snow.' Then I repeated my words of a few seconds earlier, this time with more urgency. 'I think we'd better be getting on our way.'

'All right,' Jimmy Franklin said, standing up as he finished securing his load of packs and equipment. 'I'm all ready.'

'Me too,' Whitey agreed, heading for the door. 'I'll get down outside. You two can lift the door off its hinges and pass it down to me, or simply let it fall. Then you can toss down the extra supplies and I'll stow them on our sledge. With three of us to do the hauling, Tracy might like to ride.'

'Oh, no!' she cried. 'I'm not going to be an extra weight for you three. Besides, I would probably freeze to death sitting still. I'll walk. And I'll do my share of the carrying. Which way are we going?'

Before I could answer her Whitey said, 'Toward the plateau.' He managed a grin and his eyebrows lifted momentarily from their accustomed droop. 'Sorry to anticipate you Hank, but we are heading for the plateau, aren't we?'

I nodded. 'Yes, there's something there that Ithaqua doesn't like, and what's bad for him is good enough for me!'

Whitey unbolted and threw open the damaged door of the aircraft, making as if to jump down – then froze as he stared out at our immediate surroundings. An instant later he stepped back and slammed the door shut behind him. I, too, had seen what waited for us outside, and suddenly the flesh crawled on my back with a life of its own. Obviously not all of Ithaqua's followers had stayed to see the end of his ceremonies, to watch him take his departure. They were waiting on the frozen snows of the plain outside even now, encircling the aircraft in a single row, having approached unnoticed in their white robes.

It was as I had suspected when I saw them through the binoculars; they were of an ancient Eskimo breed, the majority of them, although here and there in the surrounding circle I had seen white faces, too. But it was not the sight of these squat, flat-featured men that filled me with dread and set my flesh to creeping – they were, after all, only men. No, it was their mounts.

44

Wolves! Great white wolves as big as ponies, fanged and fire-eyed, pawed the snow with heavy pads, tongues lolling redly and hot breath condensing as it left flaring nostrils. And their silent riders sat these lupine mounts surely and with authority, arrogantly. Well, we would see about their arrogance; despite the initial dread that had filled me, we were not without weapons.

'Whitey, get the gun set up again in front of the door here,' I snapped. 'Jimmy, you're a good shot. Get into the nose with the rifle. Pull down that blanket so you can see what you're doing. Tracy, you'd better keep out of sight in the tail of the plane.'

I carefully shot out a window in the wall opposite the door, then knocked the remaining fragments of laminated glass loose from the frame. For a minute or so there was frantic activity in the confines of the plane, then an unnerving quiet. Our breathing began to form plumes, especially Tracy's, and of course she was the only one to actually suffer from the falling temperature. We waited, not wanting to precipitate matters.

From the door, which he had opened just a fraction, Whitey suddenly called out to me, 'Hank, one of the white men is making his way to the plane on foot. He's holding his hands up in the air. Doesn't appear to be armed. I think he wants to talk.'

'Let him in,' I answered. 'But watch him closely.'

Whitey swung the door open, pivoting his gun in an arc that covered a quarter of the surrounding circle. In the centre of his arc a thin-featured white man stepped forward. He was dressed in a snowy pelt that covered him head to toe. He was tall. He moved right up to the door and his head and shoulders came level with the lower sill. I kept him covered while Whitey stood up to slide the metal steps into position.

The stranger climbed the steps, lowering his head to enter, then threw back the hood of his robe and shook loose his hair. It was long and white, complementing the glacial paleness of his face in which, in complete contrast, huge dark eyes blazed with mad fervour. This was that priest I had seen at the foot of Ithaqua's altar.

As Whitey slid the steps back into their recess, closing the door again to its previous crack of an opening, I asked the stranger, 'Do you speak English?'

'I speak it,' he answered, in what I recognized as a Russian accent. 'I used to teach it, at the College of Cultural Sciences at Kiev. I also speak the languages of the Canadian Indians and the Eskimos. I am versed, too, in the tongues of Greenland, Sweden, Finland, Norway and Iceland – in all of the tongues of the lands that encroach upon the Wind-Walker's domain on Earth. Besides all these, I speak Ithaqua's tongue, which is not a tongue at all. The Snow-Thing knew this when he called me to Igarka. There I went, ostensibly to ski in the mountains, and there Ithaqua found me. Now I am the most powerful of all his priests!'

'You're a telepath, then,' I said, making it more a statement of fact than a question.

He turned to face me more fully and raised one white eyebrow. 'What would you know of telepathy?' he asked, in a voice which told me that my own talents were less than important. 'What I am – who I am – is of no consequence.' He looked round the interior of the plane. In profile, the hook of his nose gave him the look of some strange white bird of prey. His eyes became slits staring at Tracy where she huddled down in the narrow tail section. 'What I have been sent to do, however,' he continued, 'is all important!'

He pointed imperiously at Tracy: 'You, girl. You are to come with me – now!'

Before I could deny him, before I could even recover from the shock of his words, which had choked me with astonishment and rage, he turned again to me. 'You are

46

the leader here, yes? I see that it is so. The rest of your party – the three of you – all are invited to join the Brotherhood of Ithaqua.'

His black eyes seemed to burn into mine as he scrutinized me intently; then they narrowed. 'The Wind-Walker is particularly interested in your welfare. We are his people here on Borea, the Children of the Winds, and I am his messenger. You will have a short time to think about his offer. Consider it carefully; the alternative is terrible. Now I will take the girl, whom Ithaqua has found fair, and then I will return for your answer. You have three hours.'

He turned back to Tracy, a devilish smile twisting the line of his cold mouth. 'Come, girl. We go to prepare you for Ithaqua!'

Moving closer to him, I jammed my pistol into the hollow under his chin. 'What's your name, you dog?' I choked, no longer fully able to control my voice.

He drew himself up to his full height, an inch or two greater even than my own, and his eyes were like dark marbles as he answered: 'My name *was* Boris Zchakow, which is meaningless. Now I am High Priest of Ithaqua, who is not to be denied. Do you refuse to let the girl accompany me?'

'Listen, Boris Zchakow,' I answered, my mind seething with murderous thoughts. 'This girl is my sister. Neither you nor any other man – or monster – may take her where she will not go. Not while I live. You came here unarmed, so I won't kill you, not now. But if we ever meet again –'

'Then the pleasure will be mine!' he cut me off.

For a moment longer we stood face to face, then with a contemptuous gesture he turned once more to Tracy. 'Well, girl, do you want to see your brother and his friends dead, and perhaps yourself with them? Or would you not prefer to be one with Ithaqua, bride of the Snow-Thing, and live in wonder and glory forever?' His black eyes blazed insanely.

47

Tracy had come forward. Before I could make a move to stop her she reached out a trembling hand to the Russian, a peculiar, half-amazed, bemused expression on her face. He took her hand in his own pale claw – then threw back his head and screamed as though pierced through with a white-hot spike!

For a long moment his outstretched arm seemed to vibrate, as if he had taken hold of a naked high-tension cable; then he snatched back his hand and, cradling it, fell to his knees. His eyes were no longer imperious and huge but sunken black holes in a dead white face. As Tracy stepped nearer still he held up his hands before him, cringing away from her like a whipped dog. And then I understood, for the hand with which he had taken hold on her was black as pitch; the flesh curled crisply from the little finger, exposing white bone!

Tracy's face, too, had changed. Gone the bemused, hypnotized look that had fooled me, her own brother, no less than it had fooled the Russian. She again held out her hand, this time palm up, to show him one of the star-stones. Then she dangled it at the end of its chain, swinging it before Zchakow's contorted face.

'You tell Ithaqua that if he wants Tracy Silberhutte, he'll have to take these, too!' she said.

Gasping, sobbing in his pain, terror and rage, with the madness in his eyes beginning to shine out as blackly as before, the Russian slowly climbed to his feet. He held his roasted hand close to him, averting his mad eyes from the star-stone, seeking only Tracy's face as he backed toward the door.

'You –' he choked out the word. 'You *will* be Ithaqua's, I promise you!' His voice rose, bubbling with insane rage. 'And when he's done with you, if I have to wait a lifetime, then –'

'Out!' I told him. 'Now – before I kill you out of hand!'

I motioned to Whitey. He opened the door – then threw his weight against the Russian's back. With a gurgled cry of astonishment Zchakow hurtled out and down. Moments later he staggered into view on the snow and without looking back made his way to a wolf mount. He was helped onto its back and took a fistful of white mane, yanking the animal about face. He kicked the wolf's flanks, driving it in the direction of the pyramid.

Hunched over his mount's back like some nightmare hag, Zchakow threw up his head to utter a weird, ululant cry that rang loud in frozen air. As its echoes died away there came the sharp crack of Jimmy's rifle from the nose of the plane.

'Here they come!' Whitey yelled, crouching down quickly behind his machine gun. I moved to my window. And then all hell broke loose.

4

Battle on Borea

(Recorded through the Medium of Juanita Alvarez)

Out there on the plains of snow behind the advancing single rank of wolf-warriors, six white-robed priests threw up their arms to the skies and repeated the departing Russian's eerie cry. We heard that concerted wail even as we opened fire on the charging warriors – heard it and saw its result.

As the first of the advancing riders went down beneath our bullets, the grey skies of Borea began to darken over. Black clouds piled up out of nowhere and a rushing wind filled the air with loose snow. Through this whirling white screen the wolf-warriors reached the plane, dividing into two main groups, one battering at the windows of the nose while the other gathered about the door. Whitey's target was a mass of snarling wolf-masks and inscrutable, flat leathery faces. Riders stood up on the backs of their mounts, ready to leap in at us through the open door, only to find a deadly hail of lead spraying out at them from that opening. The snow of the plain in a wide area about the door began to turn red with spouting blood, animal and human alike, spilling out like scarlet pearls on a vast white feather bed. On and on the machine gun chattered its mad message of death, hot barrel swinging in a wide arc.

In the nose of the aircraft Jimmy constantly changed his position, now firing to the left, now right, and the sharp crack of his rifle was accompanied by a steady piling up of white-robed bodies and huge carcasses. In my own position, I was able to lean out of the window and pick off riders as they circled the plane trying to find vulnerable spots in our defences. But seeing that the fuselage windows were too small to admit our attackers, I quickly moved down into the plane's nose to put a shot through a window on that side away from Jimmy. Then we sat back to back. He blazed away with his rifle; I rested my pistol across my forearm as I carefully picked off my targets one by one.

It was a sickening, bloody massacre – there could be no thrill in this wholesale taking of life. And no sooner had this thought occurred to me than the wolf-warriors broke off their attack, drawing back to their previous positions away from the plane and becoming lost in the madly blowing snow. Many riderless wolves trotted after the surviving party of mounted animals.

'Hold your fire!' I cried. 'No point in wasting ammunition.' I looked around the interior of the aircraft. 'Anyone hurt?'

Grim faces turned in my direction. Thumbs up from Whitey; a cheerless grin from Jimmy. Tracy came to me and took hold of my arm. It suddenly dawned on me how cold the plane must be now – how cold Tracy must be.

'Tracy, I –'

'It's all right, Hank,' she hushed me. 'I'm fine.'

'You're sure?'

She nodded. 'I was frightened at first – of the Russian, of those wolf-things – but now I'm fine. Just a bit cold.' She blew on her hands and thrust them deep into parka pockets. 'Didn't Jimmy say that there were two pistols?'

Before I could answer her, Whitey called to me from the door. 'Hank, they're up to something. Come and have a look.'

I went to the door and peered over his shoulder. The wind still moaned like a thousand demons in pain, like all the ghosts of the spaces between the spheres, rushing here and there and flinging up the snow in our faces. Between

51

flurries I saw that Whitey was right; the Children of the Winds were definitely up to something. Having lost about twenty per cent of their number, several of the remaining riders had now dismounted. I saw one of them call over a pair of riderless animals ·and pull their great heads close – and in the next instant I understood.

'They're going to send in the wolves alone!' I yelled. The words were barely out of my mouth when a great white shape came leaping up out of the flurrying snow to slam head and forelegs in through the open door. The huge wolf hung there for a moment, yellow eyes wild above snarling gnashing fangs, scrabbling at the rubber of the floor with massive paws before falling back outside. The sight of the thing had so petrified me that I hadn't managed to get off a shot. Now I pulled myself together.

Whitey had been thrown back from his position, the machine gun too, and as he struggled to get his weapon back into place a second wolf flew at the door. I almost had the door shut when the beast landed; its wild rush and weight jammed the door wide open on bent hinges, throwing me back.

Yet another wolf leaped, sending the gun flying for a second time. The beast found a purchase with three of its great paws before I could start forward, ram my pistol in its ear and pull the trigger. The convulsing body fell back outside.

Now Jimmy had come out of the nose to help Whitey with the big gun, at the same time firing his rifle with one hand, as if it were a pistol. A snarling mask with yellow eyes appeared, framed momentarily in the opening as forepaws gripped the lower sill – then one of the eyes turned red as I fired point-blank into that grinning wolf-face. Again the door was clear, and now there came a brief lull in which I quickly reloaded my spare magazines.

But the lull was far too brief, for as Whitey finally got the machine gun back into position yet another wolf crashed into the opening of the door, scrabbling and snarling hideously as it fought to get inside. Both Jimmy and I fired simultaneously, and again a great white body toppled out of sight.

Tracy suddenly yelled and Jimmy dived past me to pump off three rapid shots at a massive white head that was tearing with slavering jaws at the frame of the broken window in the nose. As the wolf howled and jerked back its bloodied head, so the machine gun coughed back into life. With a wild glad cry Whitey traversed left and right, hurling a deadly stream of lead out into the teeth of the wind.

For several moments he fired until, realizing that this second attack had stopped as quickly as it had begun, I yelled, 'Save your shots!'

The lunatic chatter of the machine gun died away, and with it the howling of the wind seemed also to retreat, crying with a distant voice as the whirling snowflakes fell once more to the frozen plain.

'Save it,' I said yet again, unnecessarily. 'I think we've won the first round. Let's keep something for later.'

Within the space of only a few more minutes the frozen plain outside our aircraft was as still as a winter scene on a postcard. The remainder of the wolf-warriors and their mounts, and a fair number, too, of riderless wolves, stood well back and out of effective range.

And it was then, when even the smallest of the swirling snow devils had subsided, that I saw for the first time the true composition of those previously noted anomalous humps out on the great white plain. Unwilling at first to credit the evidence of my own eyes, I focused on the nearest mass with a pair of binoculars. That unnatural wind called up by Ithaqua's priests had blown much of the surface snow from the queer shape, revealing much more of its basic outline. Half of it, at least, was completely clear of the shrouding snow.

It was a ship. As a boy ships had always fascinated me. British by the style of her, there she lay on the snow, keeled over on one side like some vast, stranded whale. A vessel of heavy steel plates with powerful propellers and a reinforced steering system. At a guess, an ice-breaker of the late '20s, fashioned perhaps in the shipyards of the Wear or the Tyne and long since paid for by Lloyds of London; 'lost with all hands, somewhere inside the Arctic Circle.' Little they knew of it . . .

Again I swept the plain with my binoculars until I found another shape I recognized. And again it was the shape of a ship – a Viking dragonship!

Proudly that ancient sea-serpent prow lifted yet from the sea – albeit a sea of snow – and still a number of round, painted shields adorned the sweeping line of the hull. A *big* dragon, this ship, like Fafnir risen from deeps of frozen ocean, but the great mast was broken and the decks were awash in ice. It seemed to me as I gazed that the songs of old Norse ghosts came whispering to me across the bitter wastes, and a voice that called on Odin and screamed for red revenge.

When Jimmy Franklin's hand fell on my shoulder I started violently. 'What the –?'

'Easy, Hank,' he calmed me. 'It's just me, Jimmy. I've been using the glasses too, and I too have felt it, the aching and the loneliness. The Snow-Thing has a lot to pay for.'

I nodded. 'Yes, he has.'

'See over there,' Jimmy pointed across the gleaming plain at what looked like a large outcrop of rock jutting up through the snow and ice. 'Part of Earth's heritage, stolen by Ithaqua like a magpie might steal a bright button. What do you make of it?'

I turned my binoculars in that direction, focusing on the monolith. The view I got was not as distinct as I would have liked, but nevertheless the outlines of that tremendous *menhir* showed up clear enough to suggest the origins of the primitive but colossal artists whose work it was. Eskimo, very probably, though of no really definite ethnic lineage that I could pinpoint – that mansion-sized block of carved black basalt reeked of age.

Vague images stirred behind my mind's eye – of the gauntly gigantic carvings of Easter Island and the Temple of Ramses the Great at Abu Simbel, which would be dwarfed beside this monumental work – but I guessed, I *knew*, that it was older by far than these. Lost Mu and legendary Lomar might have raised vaguely similar colossi in those ages when the forebears of Khem and Babylon were wandering desert tribes, but this vast sculpture predated even such lost or drowned monuments as these.

Cut into many of the monolith's flat facets were larger-than-life pictures of mighty mammoths, shown mainly in attitudes of frenzied fear, flight, stampede! And beside the carved pachyderms ran men, squat aborigines carrying axes and spears, and also sabertooth tigers, massive reindeer and bison, wolves, bears and foxes. A primitive, Paleolithic panorama, wherein all the characters fled in terror of one universal enemy. And that enemy stood out suddenly in the upper areas of the massive block as finally I corrected the magnification of the binoculars until the hitherto blurred pictures came up fine and sharply etched.

Ithaqua! A crude representation, true, but no less obscene for that, the Thing that Walks on the Wind, a being known and dreaded and worshipped by the very earliest of man's forebears. Alien the Snow-Thing most certainly was, but his *conceit* was almost human. The primitives of Earth had sculpted a vast monument to his might, and he had brought it here with him to this world of snow and winds.

'I think I can understand why he wanted to bring *that* here,' Jimmy said, perhaps reading what was in my mind. 'But why the ships, why *people*? What sort of creature is Ithaqua really, and why does he, well, *migrate* between worlds, between dimensions? I've read just about all you ever collected on the Wind-Walker, Hank, but sometimes I really think that we all must be missing something somewhere.'

'I don't think we've missed much, Jimmy,' I told him. 'But there are certain things that haven't been written down yet – ideas Peaslee has been toying with, odd bits and pieces of information that the Wilmarth Foundation hasn't yet categorized, probabilities that the hunchmen have come up with – stuff like that. And since I've had to coordinate all this, well, I have ideas of my own.'

I put down the binoculars and looked to see how the others were making out. Whitey had made himself comfortable behind the machine gun. A cigarette drooped from his mouth and he appeared to be completely relaxed. His finger lay alongside his weapon's triggerguard, however, and his partly hooded eyes were sharply alert as they moved slowly over the thinned ranks of the seemingly impassive wolf-warriors. Tracy was merely a green and brown bulk in her camouflaged parka, calmly watchful where she half-reclined in a leather bucket-seat in the nose of the plane. I couldn't see her face for she had the hood of the inner parka up over her head, but her breathing made small regular plumes in the icy air.

Jimmy looked at me expectantly. 'Go on, I'm still listening,' he reminded me.

I paused for a moment to sort out my thoughts, then began to talk. 'All right, let's see if I can tell you something you don't already know.' It seemed a good idea at that, to chat about it, pass a little time until – until whatever was going to happen, happened.

'Ithaqua,' I began, 'is a horror come down the ages from the very mists of myth. He was known to the Ptetholites and his image may be found on Auderic cromlechs. The ancient peoples of all the lands adjacent to the Arctic Circle have left evidence of his being, and as recently as the early nineteenth century certain North American and Canadian Indian tribes have fashioned likenesses of him on their totems. Just such as we've seen on the totems of his worshippers here on Borea.'

'Speak up, big brother,' Tracy's voice interrupted, coming to me from the front of the plane. She inclined her head slightly in my direction. 'I'm not quite in on all of this yet, so if there's anything else I should know I'll gladly listen in.'

I nodded, pleased with her plucky acceptance of everything, and raised my voice. 'Among many other names, Ithaqua has been called "God of the Great White Silence", "the Snow-Thing", "God of the Winds", "the Death-Walker", "the Thing that Walks on the Wind", "the Strider in Strange Spaces", "the Wind-Walker" and "Lord of the Winds". Such is his fascination, his morbid attraction for various popular writers that they have created remarkably good fictions based upon the ancient legends. Algernon Blackwood, a British author of world-wide repute, no doubt fashioned his "Wendigo" on Ithaqua; and August Derleth, whose home was in Wisconsin and not so very far removed from the far northern territories, was the author of a number of extremely original and remarkable accurate stories about Ithaqua's incursions.

'He is the original air-elemental, in which every other Earthly myth and legend having regard to beings of the air has its source. The prototype of Gaoh, Chastri–Shahl, Quetzalcoatl, Negafok, Hotura, Tha'thka and Enlil, Ithaqua is given mention in the most ancient and most forbidden works known to man; and his winged totem-symbol is carved upon Geph's broken columns and crumbling stelae along with the insignia of the rest of the loathsome Cthulhu Cycle Deities. For of course Ithaqua is of the CCD, a prime elemental whose true origin is as dim and conjectural as that of the Universe itself.

'The Wilmarth Foundation believes that in forgotten prehistoric times, in ages predating Earthly life as we know and recognize it in its mundane forms, there was a battle. Earth and the Solar System formed the battle-ground. Beings of whom little is now known – super scientists named in those same forbidden books I have already mentioned as "the Elder Gods" – won the interplanetary war. The CCD, defeated but still threatening, were banished to prison environments. Mental and genetic blocks were planted upon them, imprinted *within* them, just as modern criminals are made to wear handcuffs or shackles. These blocks were designed to repeat through heredity, so that any offspring of the CCD would be imprisoned by those same restrictions no less than their forebears.

'Ithaqua was perhaps the least penalized of all the Cthulhu Cycle Deities in that he was banished to the alien star-winds which he still walks and, on Earth, to the windswept ice-wastes of the Arctic Circle and lands adjacent. In this he is the fulcrum upon which the futures of all his alien "cousins" of the cycle balance. Compara-tively free of the restrictions of the Elder Gods, he is the hope of the CCD; he is the one to whom all of the others look for eventual release from their immemorial impris-onment. And that is not his only ambition.

'Ithaqua is miscegenetic, with a taste for strong, beau-tiful white women. In this respect as in all others he is completely unscrupulous, sating his lusts whenever the mood takes him and with whatever woman is unfortunate enough to be to hand. He has already foisted children upon mankind – mated with "the daughters of Adam" – but of his progeny there are no known survivors. Three children there were that we know of, all of them born to white women; and all of them, mercifully, too alien to live. There may have been others that we don't know of, but that seems unlikely.

'Certainly, though, there have been other women out in the snows; women who have known Ithaqua's attentions without being strong enough, either physically or mentally, to suffer them and live knowing what they knew. Why, there's evidence to show that the Wind-Walker has had whole communities of worshippers in Canada, and that human sacrifices are still periodically made to him. Nearly always young, attractive women. As to why he desires children –'

'It's a terribly lonely existence,' Whitey cut in, 'walking the spaces between the spheres.'

I nodded. 'Yes, that's probably it in a nutshell.'

'That – *thing* – lonely?' Jimmy Franklin frowned. 'But loneliness is a human emotion, surely?'

'What about a swan that loses its mate?' Tracy argued, 'or a dog when his master dies? Surely that is loneliness?'

Whitey half nodded his head, half shook it in a curiously self-denying gesture. 'He *is* lonely,' he said, 'but it's a loneliness that's different from anything we could ever conceive of. And it's more than just loneliness, too. He has a definite purpose.'

'Whitey's right,' I agreed, 'I'm sure of it. It all goes back to the monster's ultimate purpose, that of freeing his hellish kith and kin. Think about it; there's only one Ithaqua, one Wind-Walker, and his ambition is to turn all of his alien, hideous cousins loose from their many prisons. Cthulhu from sunken R'lyeh, Hastur from the Lake of Hali, Yog-Sothoth from some dark dimension – oh, all of them.

'But if there were *two* such as Ithaqua, two "Things that Walk on the Winds", why, then the task would be that much easier. And if there were three – four?

'The mercy is that he is not invincible. There are weapons which work against him. We have such weapons in the star-stones from forgotten Mnar.' I looked at my hand, at the large blisters that covered my palm, and I laughed ruefully. 'True, only Tracy can handle the things, but that's a lot better than –'

'Hank!' Whitey called. I looked at him in time to see his eyebrows shoot up, then lower again quickly as he squinted down the sights of his machine gun. 'Reinforcements,' he grunted.

I jerked the binoculars up to my eyes and scanned the white plain in the direction of the pyramid altar.

Reinforcements, yes! Led by the Russian priest they came, gathering out of the ice-shrouded bases of the plain's weird hummocks. For those relics of Ithaqua's visits to Earth over eon-embracing ages were nothing less than the artificial wigwams and igloos of these Children of the Winds, provided for them by their Lord and Master, Ithaqua of the Snows. Wolf-warriors in their hundreds, and in their midst a large sledge, and upon that sledge –

'What do you make of that, Jimmy?' I asked.

'I would say it was a totem,' he answered. 'A heavy pole, lashed to the sledge and carved with faces and figures.'

'Yes,' Whitey snorted derisively, 'it would need to be a heavy pole. It *has* to be.' He looked at me and his eyebrows drooped ominously. 'It's a battering-ram!'

5

Ships of the Snow

(Recorded through the Medium of Juanita Alvarez)

As the great sledge bearing the battering-ram totem drew closer, the wolf-warriors formed a circle round our crippled airplane as before, only now they were three and four ranks deep. There must have been twelve hundred men and beasts surrounding us, and I doubted that we had enough ammunition to fire more than one shot at each of them. Even then, if every single round we fired found its target, we would still be swamped, inundated by sheer numbers.

The battering-ram was all of fifty feet long. Drawn by a dozen massive wolves in harness, with the leading pair bearing riders, it bumped roughly over the snow, jerking at the lashings that held it to the straining sledge. Cut from some giant pine the thing must have been, though as yet I had seen no tree growing on Borea, carved in designs of gods and devils, its head shaped into a blunt likeness of Ithaqua. That heavy head now pointed toward the plane, and as the wolf-warriors gave way to let the totem through their ranks its purpose suddenly became obvious. The nose of our craft was mainly of laminated glass and comparatively thin metal frames; the ram was directed straight at that fragile bubble.

'Whitey,' I said, knowing that the battle must break at any moment, 'whatever else you do, try to bring down those wolves pulling the totem. Same goes for you, Jimmy. Tracy, you give Jimmy cover; I'll cover Whitey from the door. Make all your shots count.'

Now, as the circle of wolf-warriors tightened and beasts and riders drew closer to the plane, a contingent of them gathered around the totem-bearing sledge, making the animals that pulled it much more difficult targets. Closer the sea of faces came – flat faces and copper faces, slant-eyed and straight, Eskimo, Indian and white – faces and pointed muzzles.

'If we don't cut loose soon,' Whitey breathed, 'we'll never thin them down.'

Even as he spoke the closing ranks began to move faster, human heels digging into animal flanks in a concerted spurring. From behind the wolf-warriors an eerie cry rang out in the frozen air: the wailing of the Priests of Ithaqua, begging the Wind-Walker to look favourably upon his warriors in battle.

'Here they come,' I yelled. 'Now . . . *let them have it!*'

The words were hardly out of my mouth before they were drowned by the stuttering rattle of the machine gun and the rapidly repeating crack of the rifle. Down went a dozen of the warriors escorting the battering-ram, one of them vanishing with a scream beneath the runners of the great sledge, and Whitey's roaring battle cry rang out triumphant – only to turn to a yelp of surprise as the first of the mounted Eskimos and Indians reached the plane.

A mass of white fur flashed by the jammed door; simultaneously a squat figure hurtled into the plane over the top of Whitey's deadly arc of fire. My single shot, striking the Eskimo in the chest, threw him sideways, dead before he hit the floor. Down he crashed, his fur-clad feet flopping across the barrel of the machine gun. The gun's chattering stilled at once and shapes swiftly gathered at the door. I fired point-blank into dark and light faces and slavering, snarling muzzles alike until my pistol was empty – but by that time Whitey had freed the gun.

Now he traversed the weapon, triggering it back into deadly life. But though the gun was alive its harshly uttered message was death. Death flew out through the open door in an arc, slicing into the wolf-warriors milling on the bloody snow. Whitey's attention, however, had been successfully drawn from the battering-ram; in the next instant we knew that the first stroke of that wolf-drawn totem was a telling one.

Still firing rapidly, Jimmy Franklin gave a sudden yell of warning as there came a tremendous crash from the nose of the plane. In the same second, caught unawares and in the act of reloading, I was thrown off my feet as the entire aircraft jerked violently. Whitey, firing the machine gun with one hand, somehow managed to hang on until the rocking of the plane subsided. Then the firing-pin of the machine gun fell on an empty chamber; the ammunition belt was exhausted.

I grabbed up another belt and threw it towards Whitey, kicking as I did so at a flat, oval-eyed face that appeared suddenly over the lower sill of the door. Then I was sent hurtling backward, knocked off my feet by a huge furry shape that shot in through the door with outstretched paws and bared fangs. Sprawling on my back I threw up my pistol against the pony-sized wolf crouching over me. I looked straight into the eyes of death as the beast's hideous muzzle descended. Then my bullet went in through his dripping jaws to blow out the back of his skull, lifting him from me with the shock of its impact. I rolled out of the way as the toppling, shuddering carcass collapsed with a crash where I had lain.

Through all of this it dawned on me that I had not heard the crack of Jimmy Franklin's rifle since the jarring crash when the totem struck the plane. Similarly the spitting sounds of Tracy's pistol had been absent. Now, as I leaped to my feet, the machine gun began to snarl once more to the accompaniment of Whitey's whooping. Mercifully, when the great wolf had leaped at me, it had done little more than pass over Whitey's head, causing him

63

to duck down and momentarily lose control of his weapon.

I saw this and barely had time to breath a sigh of relief before a gasp from Tracy swung me in her direction. She was spreadeagled against the curving wall of the plane, moving slowly away from the shattered nose section, staring back hypnotized at a squat white figure that moved after her with outstretched arms. She pointed her empty pistol at the Eskimo warrior, repeatedly, uselessly pulling at the trigger. Over and over she gasped my name.

At Tracy's stumbling feet, stretched on his back with a great bruise shining on his forehead, Jimmy Franklin lay, his rifle inches from hands that were limp and motionless. Faster the Eskimo moved after Tracy, black eyes glittering as he grabbed at her. In that same moment the head and shoulders of a second wolf-warrior appeared at the gaping hole where half the plane's nose had been caved in.

I aimed my pistol as carefully as my shaking hand would allow, pulled the trigger, aimed and fired again. My first shot went high, but was nonetheless effective for that. It seemed that the face of Tracy's attacker had barely flown apart, his corpse slamming backward into the nose section like a felled tree, before the second Eskimo was flying out through the gaping hole in the nose of the plane. As he went his arms flapped loosely, nervelessly, while the white furs on his upper body turned red in a sudden spouting.

I dropped to one knee beside Jimmy, snatched up his rifle and pumped off one quick shot into the wreckage of the nose section where I thought I saw a movement beyond the shattered windows. Then I slapped the downed man's face until he opened his eyes. Groggily he lifted his head from the floor and tried to get up; he was not seriously hurt.

'What happened?' he asked.

'You got a knock on the head,' I told him. 'Here, take your rifle.'

As I began to busy myself, swiftly reloading magazines for Tracy's and my own weapon, suddenly the lunatic chatter of the machine gun died. There came an abrupt, unbelievable silence; then, filling that silence, springing up all around the aircraft, came the moaning of vast winds.

Listening to that wind I felt the hair of my neck rise. I knew that it was unnatural, this wind, but I was equally sure that its source was *not* Ithaqua. This wind was – different. I felt not chill in my heart, my soul, listening to the blowing of this wind – only a sense of awe, of wonder.

'Whitey, what is it?' I cried. 'Why have you stopped firing?'

'Gun jammed,' he hoarsely answered, his hands tearing ineffectually at the breech-block mechanism of his weapon. 'Can't be fixed this side of – of Earth!'

'But what's happening?' Jimmy Franklin asked, staggering to a window.

Whitey's eyes went wide and his black eyebrows lifted. He peered out through the door and across the white wastes. The moaning of the wind grew louder, intermingled now with strange low cries of – fear? – from the horde outside. Snow blew into the shattered nose section, whirling along the inside of the plane and settling on our parkas. The wind howled more mournfully yet.

I went to the door, stood there beside Whitey and gazed out onto the plains of Borea. The wolf-warriors were lining up, reforming their ranks parallel to our battered aircraft, but their faces were turned away from the plane and they gazed as one toward the enigmatic plateau. Though the bodies of hundreds of their erstwhile fellows littered the snow, they had momentarily forgotten us and their attention was centred upon something else.

Then, from the direction of the pyramid altar, two more sledges rushed forward toward the lines of warriors. They were hauled by howling wolves that answered to the crack of Eskimo whips, and they were laden with weapons; large, tomahawk-like axes, harpoons and spears.

'I wondered where all their weaponry was,' Jimmy Franklin said. 'It looked for a while as though we were supposed to be taken alive. But now – now it looks like we're really in for it!'

Whitey studied the scene out on the snows a moment longer and his eyebrows knitted as his frown deepened. 'No, no. Those weapons are not intended for use on us.'

'What do you mean?' I questioned.

He grinned in answer, then pulled me over to the opposite window. Louder and louder howled the eerie wind, blowing now quite perceptibly from the direction of the plateau, bringing with it the sound of – *slapping sails and creaking rigging!*

'It's my hunch we're about to be rescued,' Whitey grinned again. 'Look, here comes the cavalry!'

I looked, and at first could not believe my eyes.

Down the gradual slope from the plateau they sailed, majestic and awesome on huge skis, with billowing triangular sails reaching high into whistling air – platforms with shallow hulls, upon whose decks crouched half-naked warriors amid what at first appeared to be great heaps of furs – ships, a dozen of them, sailing the snows! I snatched my binoculars up to my eyes incredulously, cursed the flurries of snow blown up by the phantom wind to obscure my vision, then finally managed to focus on one of the snow-ships.

Triple skis each perhaps forty feet long and six wide, one fore and two aft, supported the structure of the snowship's deck; the high mast was secured fore and aft, port and starboard with heavy lines. Crouching behind narrow gunwales were the warriors, wiry white bodies and squat brown ones together, gleaming with oils, eyes eager and staring straight ahead. And those piles of furs I had

66

seen – now I could make them out more clearly. Piles of fur they were indeed, but more fearsome furs a man never saw.

Suddenly one of them *stood up*, a great white mass that pawed the air and stretched itself, dwarfing its human master. Then the warrior jumped up to throw an arm about the animal's neck and pull it down again to the deck. But I had seen it, and could only gape in amazement.

A bear! They were all bears, those vast furry heaps, huge white Polar bears almost twice as big as any I ever saw in the zoos of Earth.

'The – the cavalry.' I lamely echoed Whitey's words.

'Right,' he nodded, turning to step back to the door, 'and just look at those so-called "priests" run!'

The two sledges were flying back across the snows now, back toward the pyramid altar. Emptied of their weapon loads, now they carried the priests of Ithaqua three to a sledge. Like rats from a sinking ship. 'No fighters, those priests,' Whitey muttered.

'Jimmy,' I swung about, an idea forming in my mind. 'How do you feel?'

'I think I'm all right,' he answered, gingerly fingering his bruise. 'An almighty headache, that's all.'

'And you, Tracy?'

'Fine, Hank,' her voice began to tremble, then steadied. 'But what's on your mind?'

'Whitey reckons that these ships and their crews are here to dig us out of this mess we're in. I say let's make their job a bit easier. We can perhaps leave the plane and fight our way over to the men of the ships. If they are here to pull us out of the fire, they'll be able to disengage that much earlier and take us back to the plateau. Who's for it?'

All three nodded as one person; then Whitey reminded, 'We have only three guns among us.'

'We'll keep Tracy in the middle,' I answered. 'Form a triangle around her. Jimmy keeps his rifle; you and I, Whitey, have the pistols.'

'And all these supplies of ours, that we planned to take with us?' Jimmy asked.

'They may still come in handy,' I told him. 'We'll take them.'

The three of us tugged and wrestled at the door while Tracy urged us on. Finally we forced it from bent hinges, letting it fall onto the reddened snow outside. We quickly threw down our belongings and equipment, then jumped down ourselves. Tracy came last, dropping into Jimmy's arms.

Now we could clearly hear the swish of the great skis and the crack of snapping sails. Hurrying around under the tail of our crippled aircraft, loaded down with equipment and hauling a sledge heaped high with bundles, we caught our first glimpse of the two factions as they faced up to one another.

The snow-ships were still now, twelve of them in a line, sails already half-furled and decks half-cleared; and the gleaming warriors who had crowded those decks were mounting massive bears on the plain and moving their mounts into a tight formation. Men and bears; a fearful army, a fantastic sight!

In their right hands the fighting men of the ships carried lances, and swinging from their leather waist-belts were picklike weapons, polished bright. The bears, of course, required neither arms nor armour; their furs were thick and their hides tough, and their terrible claws were the most lethal weapons for hand-to-hand fighting that I had ever seen. The two armies of warriors, both double-ranked now, moved toward each other. Fur-clad Eskimo, Indian and white man, spurring on their huge wolves; face to face with men of similar origins but different ideals and creeds, mounted on massive Polar bears. The armies moved closer, seemed to poise for an instant of time on the white plains of Borea, then rushed together in the clash and roar of terrible battle!

In a moment the double line of wolf-warriors broke and the bears surged through the gap, tearing all apart that stood in their way. But for all their giant strength and determined ferocity, not all of them won through. I saw one bear go down, hamstrung by the slashing claws of a great wolf; but even as the Eskimo rider of the bear fell, so he hurled his weapon at a mounted, copper-coloured wolf-warrior. Such was the force of the Eskimo's hurled lance that even striking its target a glancing blow it lifted the Indian from his wolf's back. In another second the two unseated men were hand-to-hand, and in the next the squat man of the snow-ships had driven his bright picklike weapon through the proud hawk face of the redskin wolf-warrior. Then the battle surged over that gory, heroic scene and it was lost to me.

We ran as best we could toward the break in the ranks of the Children of the Winds, hauling our sledge behind us, keeping close together and forming a knot around Tracy. As we went we fired our weapons at the closest of the wolf-warriors and their mounts. We had been spotted as we left the plane and this closest group of our previous attackers was already fighting its way desperately toward us; the wolf-warriors did not intend to let us go so easily. Then additional orders were given by someone behind us, from the direction of the distant pyramid.

A strange, drawn-out ululation sounded, and it caused a greater contingent of the fighting wolf-warriors to wheel about face and come racing back toward us!

Cursing the utterer of that cry out loud, glancing back as I urged the other three on to the spitting song of the pistols and the cracking tune of Jimmy Franklin's rifle, I saw a sleek sledge knifing over the plain. The crusty snow flew in a white sleeting as bright runners cut through it, crushed it, hurled it aside. Six massive wolves hauled the sledge at a loping run, labouring under the whip of an Eskimo driver, and holding to the skimming vehicle's chariotlike prow crouched a half-dozen of the fiercest, largest men I have ever seen. Giants all, only three of these prime warriors were Eskimo; two others were copper-skinned Indians, the last a white man.

Ah, yes. And behind them crouched the utterer of that ululant alarm: Boris Zchakow, the fanatic, wind-maddened Russian. Ithaqua's number one priest. Behind Zchakow's sledge sped two others recently fled, returning again with their complement of lesser priests; and bringing up the very rear, at a distance of about a mile, as many wolf-warriors again as I had yet seen.

Twelve, no fifteen hundred of them. All armed and hurtling pell-mell in a strong, wedge-shaped formation, harpoons and spears tilted forward – and then, even as we threw ourselves to one side to sprawl on the frozen snow, the runners of the leading sledge hurled ice in our faces as it careened past. The six great warriors leaped from it to rush upon us. Now I could see that they carried metal shields – and huge metal tomahawks!

Crouching low, advancing with their weapons held high, they closed in a circle backed by a dozen wolves and their riders. From my prone position I could see the Russian priest's face. His eyes were triumphantly ablaze as, behind the advancing warriors, he peered over the prow of the now stationary sledge.

'Zchakow, you dog!' I yelled, firing one quick shot in his direction. I saw splinters fly from the sledge's woodwork near his face, then was forced to turn my weapon to more immediate work. Almost upon us, at point-blank range, was a furclad giant, then a second. My first shot clanged harmlessly off metal, the second took its target full in the throat above the giant's shield. This was the white man, towering at least seventy-eight inches and broad-bodied, screaming bubblingly and clawing at his scarlet throat as he went down in a welter of blood. Far from deterring the remaining five warriors, my shots seemed to spur them on. They leaped forward –

Jimmy Franklin's weapon had more penetrating power than the two pistols; crouching, he now slammed round after round into whichever target presented itself. Two of the huge Eskimos and an Indian fell, gaping holes showing in both shields and bodies. A pair of the wolf-warriors, too, reeling bloodily from their mounts. My own and Whitey's weapon both were taking their toll in support of the rifle, but they were simply not enough. Spears flew; the warriors rushed in; tomahawks flashed –

Knocked down, I rolled, and hearing a shrill scream from Tracy bounded back to my feet. Whitey was down, struggling with the shaft of a spear where it pinned his thigh to the snow. A great arm had snatched my sister aloft to throw her across a broad, fur-draped shoulder. I fired a bullet straight into the heart of the hawkfaced redskin who held her struggling form, heard his scream as he toppled.

Tracy fell beside me, winded and sobbing. Whitey had passed out flat on the snow. Jimmy Franklin's hoarse cry rang out, bringing me whirling about in a crouch to seek a new target. None was near. Some way off stood the single remaining giant Eskimo. I aimed at him carefully and pulled the trigger. The hammer fell on an empty chamber.

Now I saw that Jimmy deliberately held his fire, noticed that the special force of wolf-warriors had fallen back along with the sole surviving giant. And yet still the Russian priest roared with rage from the safety of the sledge. Without understanding a single word of the language he spoke I knew that he goaded them on, calling them cowards and heaping all kinds of insults upon them. But they were not listening to him, and though they were suddenly fearful I knew that it was neither fear of my pitifully small party nor of our marvellous weapons that stayed them.

They stared at something behind us, *above* us – stared open-mouthed, wide-eyed – fearfully! They lowered their weapons and backed still farther away from us, a lone foot-soldier springing into the saddle of a riderless wolf; and all the time they stared, yes, and they *listened*.

In another second the mad Russian's roaring stopped abruptly as he, too, looked beyond and above us, stared and listened. Now there was an amazing hush as the armies froze in the midst of bloody battle. Slowly we turned our heads, Tracy, Jimmy and I. We looked in the direction of the plateau.

Part Two

1

Woman of the Winds

(Recorded through the Medium of Juanita Alvarez)

Staring at the sky above the low, ominous outcropping of the plateau, I thought: *One of two things: either these people have especially sensitive hearing, or they are accustomed to listening for things that I would not normally expect to hear.*

But then I did hear it; a whirling of high winds, a great tumult in the heavens of Borea whose physical effects could not for the moment be felt on the plain where I stood. Then, slowly but surely, the whirling became a rushing, a roaring as of a swollen river.

Since the battle on the plain first began the skies had been piling up with cloud. Over the plateau the air was dark and writhing, pulsating as if alive; and now, in the centre of this chaos, there formed a circle of madly spinning black cloud like a slice cut through the upper stem of a tornado.

Weirdly that disc of frenzied vapour tilted toward us and with quickening pace, independent of all other atmospheric formations, sped across the lowering skies. Such was its independence that all other clouds, large and small, fled to clear a grey path for it that led straight across the heavens! Strangely, seeing that clearing of the sky-path, the stricken wolf-warriors were mortally afraid, while I personally felt great awe but no fear. Neither did the men of the snow-ships nor my own small team, although judging by the gasps of amazement from the latter they were as much in awe of this fantastic sight as I was.

Tilting my head up higher, I followed the flight of the disc of whirling cloud along the sky-path until it slowed and stopped almost immediately overhead. And now a vast and gasping sigh, composed of a mass moaning from the wolf-warriors and a concerted, ecstatic exhalation from the rest, went up from the hypnotized tableau on the plain. In the next moment, as if a spell had been lifted by that sighing murmur of the armies, the battle resumed.

But now there was a difference, for from the instant of resumption the battle progressed clearly in favour of the men of the snow-ships. The wolf-warriors fought as they retreated, true, but their lines were bending like grass before a breeze as they milled back from the swaggering bears and their jubilant riders, and to a man they seemed to keep one eye on the sky overhead – on the sky, and on the ominous black disc that whirled and roared above us.

Seeing that the battle was rejoined and having clipped a fresh magazine into my pistol, I prepared to defend myself once more. I crouched beside Tracy where she huddled over Whitey's still form, trying to free the spear that pinned his leg to the frozen surface. Whitey's pistol, flown from his hand when he fell, was nowhere to be seen.

Jimmy Franklin, out of ammunition, had reversed his rifle and now gripped the barrel with both hands like a club. For a moment we stared at each other, Jimmy and I, and then he said, 'Hank, it looks to me like these people here are scared to death – almost as scared as I am. This could be our chance to make a break for the snow-ships.'

He was right. The circling wolf-warriors had pulled farther back from us; much closer were the advancing lines of fighting bears, cutting off our attackers from the rest of the wolf-warrior pack. I handed Tracy my pistol, put both hands to the shaft of the spear (mercifully a true spear and not a barbed harpoon) that fastened Whitey down, and pulled it free as smoothly and gently as I could.

Whitey moaned and trembled on the frozen ground. Tracy handed the pistol back to me and sat down to cradle Whitey's head, wiping his brow with snow.

Jimmy Franklin threw down his useless rifle and reached for the bloodied spear. 'All right,' I told him, 'we'll make a break for it. I'll carry Whitey; Tracy will have to stay between us.'

Then, before we could make our move – even above the crazed rushing and roaring of the whirling black disc hanging above us, over the clash of battle and the screams of dying men and beasts – again the mad Russian priest's scornful voice rang out, lashing our ring of attackers into activity.

But no, despite the fact that they obviously feared this wild-eyed white man, the warriors would have none of it. True, they made a half-hearted show of rushing upon us, but as soon as my pistol resumed its vicious spitting they spurred their wolves to a hurried retreat. And now they were gathering into a group, no longer ringing us, backing away in the direction of the distant pyramid altar and prepared at any moment to turn and flee.

It could have been that their reluctance was due to the fact that the men of the snow-ships were now breaking through the disordered wolf-warrior lines in a dozen different places, but I was sure that it was much more than this, that it still had a lot to do with the whirling disc in the maddened sky. But now, however hesitantly, indecisively, massive wolf-warrior reinforcements were arriving to bolster the faltering morale of their bat-'tered brothers. Well over a thousand of them, these were the men of that wedge-shaped formation I had seen bringing up the rear behind the three sledges of the priests. They paused momentarily before entering the battle.

It was at that moment that the insane Russian, wearied now of trying to goad his men to the attack, grabbed the Eskimo driver of his sledge by the arm and screamed a harsh command into his ear. Immediately the squat driver leaned forward to crack his whip across the backs of the six harnessed wolves.

Round in a semicircle the heavy sledge skidded, while Zchakow clung like a great white leech to its prow. Now, as the team of wolves hurtled straight toward us, I saw that it was the Russian's intention simply to run us down. I yanked Tracy to her feet and thrust her away, slipping and stumbling over the snow.

The sledge of the high priest hissed down upon us, and again he screamed a harsh command. In answer to that urgent cry, spurring his wolf forward out of a milling, snarling crush of human and animal bodies, rode that massive Eskimo survivor of the six warriors Zchakow had sent against us. Straight for Tracy the giant guided his massive mount, leaning out to reach for her with avid, grasping hands.

'Tracy!' I yelled. 'Tracy – *look out!*'

And at that precise instant of time, simultaneous with my cry, came a fantastic intervention. Twin, deafening reports sounded from the sky, a double-barrelled blast like that of some cosmic shotgun.

High in the heavens, emanating from the centre of the whirling disc of cloud, two great dazzling bands of fire reached out, curling over and down, swaying above the plain like twin serpent heads before leaping earthward to flash unerringly to their targets. Magnificent, awesome, fearfully *sentient* they were – thunderbolts that crashed down with pin-point accuracy upon those who would destroy us!

When they were almost upon us, suddenly the wolves that hauled Zchakow's sledge were enveloped in crackling white flame that reached from the sky. One second they were there, caught in that awful holocaust of electrical energies, and the next second that pillar of fire was gone and they were ashes through which the sledge, its prow blazing, careened to spill onto its side.

Two figures were thrown like rag dolls onto the snow: the Russian and his Eskimo driver. The latter got to his knees – just in time to catch a stray spear full in the back. The shaft ran him through, knocking him face down and stone dead upon the frozen ground. It was just as well for him that he died that way. He had been screaming hideously even before the spear hit him, and I had seen that his arms ended in steaming, redly dripping stumps at the elbows. Reaching over the prow of the sledge, those arms of his must have been caught in that same pillar of flame that incinerated the wolves.

But what of Zchakow? Where was he now? Then I saw him, mounting a riderless wolf, in a hurry to make good his escape. I lifted my weapon and had him fairly in my sights when a stumbling figure fell against me, deflecting my aim. It was Tracy, weakly calling my name, half-fainting with shock and terror.

'Oh, Hank, Hank – it was *terrible*!' she cried. I tried to clasp her to me but she pulled free to point shudderingly at a pile of smouldering fur and grey ashes on the snow: the remains of the giant Eskimo warrior and his mount. 'That fire – that awful fire from the sky!'

'Come on!' Jimmy Franklin suddenly cried. 'Now we can make it!'

I saw that he was right; the tide of battle had washed by us. Apart from a narrow strip of frozen plain littered with dead and dying men and animals, nothing now stood between us and the line of motionless snow-ships.

I threw Whitey across my shoulders and Jimmy picked up Tracy. As we stumbled toward the snow-ships a quartet of massive bears lumbered forward, their riders holding out brawny arms to us. Tracy was taken from Jimmy by a black-haired, hawkfaced man who could only be of pure Indian stock, possibly Tlingit or Chinook. She clung to him grimly as his huge mount turned about. Ten or eleven feet tall, a second bear approached me. At the command of its Eskimo rider, this moving mountain of fur lifted Whitey from my back to tuck him under a massive limb. Yet another rider reached down a hand to me, and as I swung up beside him I saw the fourth pick up Jimmy. Then we were off at a lumbering run for the nearest ship of the snow.

As we reached the ship, willing hands reached down to lift us aboard from the backs of the bears. The deck was of rough planking, along which we were hurried to the upward-sweeping prow. Whitey was borne away to the rear of the ship; I assumed that his wound was to be given immediate attention.

Tracy was on her own feet again by then, and as we gathered at the rail of the bird-beaked prow to watch the battle from this point of higher elevation, so Jimmy Franklin struck up a conversation with the stern-faced brave whose arms had lifted my sister from him. They spoke slowly at first, Jimmy finding his way with the Koluscha-Tlingit tongue, but soon the conversation became an excited babble. Shortly Jimmy held up his hand to still the tongue of his new friend; he turned to me.

'He says that we showed great courage in defying Ithaqua, and that we have done the people of the Plateau a great service in ridding Borea of so many of Ithaqua's people. He welcomes us aboard the ship of Northan the Warlord, where we await the coming of Armandra, the Woman of the Winds.'

'Hold on, Jimmy,' I told him. 'Let's take it slowly. Is your friend here this, er, Northan the Warlord? And who is Armandra?'

Again they engaged in the obscure Indian dialect, then, 'No, this is not Northan; his name is Kota'na, and he is the

Keeper of the Bears. Northan is a man like you – and yet not like you. He has your height and your blue eyes, but he is darker skinned and his hair is jet.'

'And Armandra?' Tracy asked him.

Jimmy lifted his eyes to stare out over the battle that still raged on the white plain, then turned them skyward to that enigmatic disc of madly spinning darkness. 'He says that Armandra is Priestess of the Plateau, the Woman of the Winds.' He paused, then lifted an unsteady hand to point at the whirling disc. 'And he says that Armandra is – *there*!'

'Look!' Tracy cried. 'Hank, what's happening?'

Decimated, the ranks of wolf-warriors had drawn back to form triple lines of perhaps four hundred and fifty men mounted, and another two hundred or so riderless wolves. Behind them, spaced out along the line they formed, Ithaqua's six lesser priests leaped and cavorted on the snow, their cries reaching us on the wings of a wind that suddenly rose up to blow from the distant altar into the faces of the warriors of the snow-ships. Behind the six priests, raised high atop a human pyramid of white-robed warriors, Boris Zchakow held up his arms to the skies and offered up a cry the like of which I was sure civilized man never heard before from throat of man.

Close about us pressed a dozen or so of the half-naked men of the ships, murmuring excitedly, expectantly, staring out across the plain. Jimmy Franklin asked a further guttural question of Kota'na and on receipt of the answer again turned to me.

'He says that Ithaqua's priests are fools; that while their master is undisputed "First Lord of the Winds", Armandra's powers are second only to his, and that any forces the priests can call up will be child's play for the Woman of the Winds. And such tomfoolery, he says, will only anger her. Look!'

As he spoke he flung out an arm to point across the battlefield. About two hundred yards of death-littered plain separated the two armies. Now, between them and growing up out of the frozen ground in front of the ranks of wolf-warriors, six towering tornadoes reached skyward. Thin spirals at their bases, thickening at their tops to about one hundred feet in diameter, they whirled like spinning tops, gathering up all of the loose surface rime of the plain and rapidly becoming almost solid cones of snow and ice.

Then, with almost military precision, these evocations of an alien science began to move forward toward the opposing army. As they crossed the open space the bodies of fallen men and beasts – Eskimo, Indian, Mongol and European, and the carcasses of wolves and bears alike – were swept up into their funnels to whirl madly in the tumult of frozen debris.

Now those six priests also moved forward, advancing between the wolf-warriors, urging their fantastic, inhuman charges on with cries and crazed cavortings. All of this I saw through the binoculars which I still wore round my neck, but soon I could no longer hear the cries of those priests for they were utterly drowned out in the torrent of sound that washed outward from the awesome scene on the plain.

Staunchly stood the men and bears of the ships, unfaltering in a whipping wind that threatened to blow them all away like leaves in a gale, facing the whirligigs of doom that rushed upon them. And then a gasp went up from the figures that crowded me in the prow of the snow-ship. In the sky above the armies, something was happening.

Dead centre in the whirling disc of black cloud an opening had appeared, and down through this opening a shape now lowered – a human shape. No, perhaps not human, for how could any person of flesh and blood be up there, walking down the wind beneath that enormous aerial Catherine-wheel? And yet, unless my own eyes played games with me, that figure was indeed human – the gorgeous shape of a woman whose flesh was as white as the snow of the plain – a woman garbed in white fur boots and a short fur smock, who fell in a swift but *controlled* motion down through the air with her arms held wide and parallel to the ground, forming a living cross. Her hair was billowing above her, long and flaming red, rippling as she fell like the tail of some fiery meteorite of flesh.

Down she came, slowing to a gradual halt, still as a hawk on the wind, level with and facing the flat caps of the viciously spinning tornadoes. She stood in thin air, surveying the scene before and beneath her with lowered head. Her back was toward us and her face hidden, but nevertheless I knew she must be beautiful. Beautiful and regal – and powerful.

Now she moved her arms out toward the six white titans that threatened her with their spinning, nodding heads, palms flat against them, denying them – and they paused in their forward motion as if suddenly come up against an invisible wall. Trembling and swaying wildly, fighting to move forward against the will of that Woman of the Winds, the great spinning tops strove to obey the ecstasies of the priests behind them. But her will was stronger than theirs, stronger than the combined wills of all the priests of Ithaqua together.

Faster the tornadoes whirled, frenziedly battering themselves against the invisible wall of Armandra's will, gyrating erratically and losing all of that precision with which they had marched across the plain. Their end was quick; unable to move forward they began to sway from side to side, falling one against the next like dominoes tumbling in a row, and since they could not tumble forward they fell back the way they had come.

And that was a sight to remember, the tumbling and crashing of those nearly solid inverted cones of snow and ice. An avalanche from the sky, the collapsing columns smashed down to raise a thick haze of ice-dust that momentarily obscured the panic gripping the wolf-warrior army. How the Priests of Ithaqua escaped with their lives in that shattering deluge I could never say, but escape they did, for when the white haze began to settle they were already aboard their sledges, and Boris Zchakow with them, rushing back across the white waste toward the distantly towering pyramid altar.

With my binoculars I found the mad Russian, saw him turn to glare, eyes bulging, at the figure of the woman in the sky, mouthing some unheard obscenity and shaking a fist at her in lunatic fury.

Ah, the fool – for Armandra saw him too!

The flaming hair of that fantastic figure billowed up on her head and seemed to glow with an unnatural light, turning her whole body and the simple garment she wore a peculiar copper colour, like frozen gold. Slowly, deliberately, she reached up one slender arm above her head and the chill copper glow extended from her pointing hand to spiral upward to the great disc of black cloud that yet whirled and roared above her, a primal watchdog guarding its mistress.

She began to rotate her arm, the circle rapidly growing wider as if she twirled the rope of some enormous lasso. And the cloud-disc, the loop of that lasso, spun with her arm, speeding up until its edges became a wispy blur laced with flickering traceries of electrical fire.

Now the wolf-warrior army was in full flight, hurtling away down the slight slope toward the distant circle of totems and its central altar. Totally disarrayed, chaotic, theirs was a panic flight which, like a stampede, would not be checked until men and beasts had run themselves out. They were done with fighting for this day, hurrying home to lick their wounds and count their dead; and riding with them in their midst went Boris Zchakow, head and shoulders taller than the three men who rode his sledge with him.

From this fleeing rabble back to the Woman of the Winds my binoculars flew, and now I could almost feel the anger radiating from her where she stood in coppery splendour atop the very air. '*Zchakow*,' I told the distant madman under my breath, '*Russian – if you think you have an enemy in me, you don't know the half of it. Human enemies you can possibly afford, but not such as this Woman of the Winds!*'

And oh, I was right.

Now the figure in the sky seemed to swell outward, burning bronze to match the billowing tresses that crowned her – and for a moment I thought I knew where I had seen a similar *expansion* before. But then, in another moment, the shape was human again, only human.

Human? I laughed at myself derisively. There must be that in this being which was human, yes, but there was more, much more than that to her. There was this power of hers over the elements – and there was her anger.

Now she lowered that slender arm of hers to a horizontal position, and the great disc above her head tilted forward, dipped, slid down the wind, rushed like some gigantic discus thrown by a god in the Games of Heaven – or a demon in hell's chaos. Levelling out over the white waste, it rushed after the fleeing army of wolf-warriors.

Tracy clutched my arm, her breath pluming faster as she watched that incredible scene. 'Oh, Hank – how *could* she?'

It was one thing to be engaged in a fight for one's life with fallible, mortal enemies, but another thing entirely to see this Woman of the Winds, this being who fought with weapons fashioned of the forces of nature, ruthlessly, cold-bloodedly destroy a small army.

And surely that army, or what was left of it, would be destroyed if the whirling juggernaut Armandra had unleashed upon it were allowed to run amuck through its scattered, fleeing ranks.

'I – I don't know,' finally I answered Tracy's question, surprised to find that my throat was dry and my voice cracked.

'They are terrible people,' Tracy continued, 'but they *are* people!' Then she closed her eyes and turned her face to me as the great disc caught up with the hindmost of the fleeing wolf-warriors.

Unable to tear my eyes away from the scene, I felt my lips draw back in a gasp of horror as the disc struck, tearing into and ripping through men and beasts as the blade of a circular saw rips wood, flinging the debris of its passing hundreds of feet into the icy air and across the white waste. And then, even as I watched, the disc paused, hesitated.

With shaking hands I focused yet again upon the Woman of the Winds. Now she had thrown up an arm before her eyes, her other hand thrust out before her as if to ward off some unseen horror – the horror of her own inhuman anger unleashed. In the next instant she shook her head, sending her magnificent red tresses billowing, then waved her arms outward in a sharp, clear sign of dismissal.

And suddenly there was a tremendous roaring from the plain, such as a tidal wave might make breaking on some unsuspecting promontory. The weapon she had hurled at the fleeing army flew apart, disintegrated, returned in the space of a few seconds to its elemental form, lay as inert over the plain as a grey cloud! A cloud that settled to a ground haze, revealing at last the hundred or so remaining wolf-warriors racing frenziedly on beyond its drifting, curling tendrils.

Faintly, breaking the sudden silence, reaching us on a mournful wind that sprang up in the wake of all that had

passed, came a distant rumbling and hysterical screaming from the spared, fleeing wolf-warriors. For certainly
Armandra had spared them, and I knew now that there
was more of the human in her than I had suspected.

'She let them go!' breathed Tracy.

'Let them go!' Jimmy Franklin gasped, echoing her, his
voice clearly displaying relief.

'Yes she did,' said another well known voice, edged now
with pain, from behind us.

It was Whitey, hobbling on one leg, his arm around the
fat neck of a grinning Eskimo. 'She did, so there's hope
for her yet,' he finished.

'Whitey, what do you mean?' I asked.

He nodded grimly in answer, eyebrows lowering, staring
at the figure of the woman in the sky. 'See for yourself,'
he said.

As a tremendous accolade of cheering, whooping, and
the rattling of hundreds of weapons on shields went up
from the victorious army of the snow-ships, I looked up
and saw – and understood. I understood this woman's
power over the elements of the air, her ability to walk
on the wind, her inhuman anger and her all-too-human
anguish.

For now she had turned to face her people, and hearing
their wildly clamorous applause she held out her slender
arms to them. Her marvellous hair swirled above her and
her eyes shone momentarily as a great queen's to the
ringing cheers of her subjects.

Her eyes shone, then for the space of a single instant
blazed bright carmine, twin stars in her regal face!

Whitey nodded again, then said, 'The safest hunch I
ever had in my life, Hank. That woman is without doubt
a child of Ithaqua, and we must thank our lucky stars that
she appears to have broken away from her monstrous
father!'

2

On the Ship of Northan

(Recorded through the Medium of Juanita Alvarez)

Half an hour later, during which time the ski-borne ships were brought about and the great bears paraded up onto their decks to be chained to individual rings, the last few wounded men and animals were being brought aboard when Armandra herself took her place at the prow of this ship of her warlord.

During that interval we had also met Northan the Warlord, if it could be called a meeting. A big man, tall as myself and muscled about his arms and shoulders like one of the bears, he had paused momentarily in the issuing of multilingual commands to stride to the prow of the ship and look us over. He literally did that; looked us over, and the frown of disdain that grew on his darkly handsome face told me that he hardly considered us worth the effort.

I immediately, irrationally, took a dislike to him. Blue-eyed with light brown skin and long dark hair, his face and form seemed to me to hold elements of many races, a powerful lineage.

My dislike increased by leaps and bounds when he casually chucked Tracy under the chin, lifted her head and grunted grudgingly. Before I could say or do anything he had strode away again, but from then on I watched him more closely; not because I believed that Tracy needed a watchdog, but simply because I don't like being held in any sort of contempt. The man who does that to me or mine must then live up to it.

I was still thinking dark and as yet unjustified thoughts when finally Armandra came aboard. Her arrival at the prow of the snow-ship was as awe-inspiring as anything we had seen of her yet, for of course she walked down the wind to step aboard the vessel from an invisible platform of air that buoyed her up as if she were a bubble.

Watching Northan as he strode the deck issuing his orders and pointing here and there with the stock of a short whip, I turned only in time to see her take the last step that brought her aboard – from a position some fifteen to twenty feet above the frozen surface of the plain! – and I would have missed even that last step but for the sudden gasp that went up from the vessel's crew. That and the fact that all around me men were falling to their knees, heads bowed in absolute reverence. Kota'na went down instantly, dragging Jimmy Franklin with him unprotesting; even Whitey knelt, though it brought a moan of pain to his lips to have to bend his wounded leg. I couldn't see Tracy for she stood slightly to my rear, but I later learned that even she had humbly lowered her head; Tracy, as proud a girl as ever walked.

Without any shadow of doubt this Woman of the Winds had magic; a magic which, while my body must ever stay rooted to earth, was nevertheless powerful enough to send my soul walking on air. Oh, yes, she was beautiful, this Armandra.

Draped as she was in a white fur smock, still her long full body was a wonder of half-real, half-imagined curves that grew out of the perfect pillars of her white thighs. Her neck, framed now in the red silk of her tresses, was long and slender, adorned with a large golden medallion.

I have never been much of a poet, and no less could do justice to her face. It was the face of an angel; oval and beautifully moulded, white as snow. In it great green eyes – mercifully green where once I had seen them glow red – stared out from beneath fine golden eyebrows that lay straight and horizontal beneath a high brow. Her nose was straight, too, but delicate and rounded at its tip, while her mouth was curved in a perfect, if a fraction too ample, cupid's bow.

Hair red as fire and eyes green as the deep northern seas of Earth, and a skin as white and smooth as the snowy marble of quarries of dream; this was Armandra's face. And as I gazed at that face I saw one eyebrow lift a little, wonderingly, and the smallest of smiles beginning to –

– And then I was knocked from my feet by a charging blow to my shoulder that would have brought down an ox! I went flying, to crash jarringly against the rail of the prow where I fell to my knees. The next moment Northan appeared over me, legs spread wide and eyes blazing.

I knew immediately that the warlord's anger sprang from my apparently irreverent attitude toward the Woman of the Winds, in which he could not in fact be more mistaken. Indeed, I already revered this woman, but not as any religious worshipper. Snarling and blustering the bully raised his whip, and as I came to my feet he snapped the thing to send its single metal-tipped thong flying in my face. How easily he might have caught my eye, but instead the metal cut me high on the cheek – and higher still on my pride. Pride goes before a fall they say, but be that as it may this time it would be Northan's fall. On that I was determined.

I reached up a hand to my face to feel a thin trickle of blood, and I felt my eyes widen and the skin about my mouth tighten involuntarily. Northan's arm went back again – and immediately a chiming voice rang out. Too late that golden voice of imperial command, for already the whip was snapping, and I was moving forward inside its wicked radius.

As the metal-tipped thong flew harmlessly over my shoulder I turned slightly to one side and drove my elbow deep into Northan's body below his ribcage. He bent over, almost double, and as he expelled air in a great gasp of surprise, so my cupped hands, clenched into a hard knot, rose up to strike his descending brow.

Most men would have died there and then, of a fractured skull or broken neck, but not Northan the Warlord. His neck was like that of a bull. The shock of the blow I had delivered nearly broke my arms as my opponent's body lifted clear from the planking, flew across the narrow prow and smashed through the opposite rail. He spun out of sight and fell to earth. The fact that I had not killed him was all too obvious from the cry of disbelieving rage that swelled up a moment later from below, and in the outraged bellow that followed as the warlord came limping up the wide gangplank amidships his dark face working and a picklike weapon gleaming in his fist.

But again Armandra's bell-like tones rang out, and this time she spoke in English. 'Stop this now, Northan! You should be ashamed of yourself, thus to treat a man who has fought so well against Ithaqua's wolf-warriors. And you –' she turned her now wrathful eyes on me, 'to attack the man whose army has saved all of your lives!'

'I only returned his blows,' I answered, neither liking this chastisement nor yet quite knowing how to answer it.

'My brother allows no man to strike him.' Tracy's sweet, angry voice came from beside me as Northan swung himself up onto the raised platform. 'The warlord must consider himself lucky to be alive!'

I had to grin at my sister's pluck and her faith in me; and I saw now that Armandra also smiled at Tracy, that her smile widened noticeably as she said, 'Your brother? I had thought perhaps that –'

'You, man, stand and fight!' came Northan's rage-filled, guttural voice. He crouched before me on the raised deck, eyes red with fury, picklike weapon grasped tightly in a massive, bloodless hand.

'Northan!' the Woman of the Winds gasped. 'I have told you that –'

'But Armandra, he refused to kneel before you, and struck me with his naked hands when I would have punished him! The dog must –'

'He struck fair blows when you should have expected them, and they were telling blows,' she taunted him. 'And where you used a weapon, he did not, though his weapon,' she indicated the pistol at my waist, 'could have killed you instantly.'

For a moment longer we stood there, the three of us, in some sort of confrontation. Then, 'Enough,' the Woman of the Winds cried. 'It is done now, finished. We are wasting time and no one knows when Ithaqua might return to Borea.' She fingered the medallion she wore about her neck, seeming suddenly nervous. 'It is time we were away. I will call a wind to blow us home to the plateau.'

The dark frown stayed on Northan's face, but as Armandra spoke he lifted his head and sniffed the air. 'It's much too quiet,' he finally rumbled in agreement. 'Can you not see, Armandra, what Ithaqua's devils are up to?'

'No, not now,' she shook her head. 'I need my strength to call the wind. Today's work was hard.'

So saying, she stepped into the very point of the prow, lifting up her arms until she resembled some perfectly carved figurehead. As she assumed that posture her red tresses eerily floated up over her head, while tiny gusts of wind sprang up from nowhere to play with the fur collar of her smock. A moment later the great, loosely hanging sails began to fill out. Behind us, far back across the death-strewn white waste, a hundred snow-devils grew up from the frozen ground to race toward us, lifting into the air and swirling themselves into nothingness.

And then the wind came, moaning in tune to the sudden groaning of the rigging and the creaking of straining timbers, and we were off with a lurch and a slither and a hissing of huge skis, riding the snow-ship of Northan the Warlord back to its berth in the base of the plateau. Gracefully the great ships slid into an arrowhead formation, and the wind Armandra had called blew us steadily away from the scene of the recent battle.

Oh, there were sights to be seen and thrills to be experienced during that short, strange voyage, no doubt about that; but for me – I could not take my eyes off the figure of the not-quite-human woman-creature who stood so proudly in the prow with her hair floating weirdly over her head and her slender arms held up to feel the loving caress of currents of air. And I envied those gentle currents whose soft fingers caressed her. The others – Tracy, Whitey and Jimmy – they could watch the sailors of the snow-ship about their tasks, speculate on the origins of the many tongues they heard, thrill to the sway of the deck and the strange odours of men and beasts. For my eyes there was only Armandra.

After a while she must have felt my eyes upon her for she turned her head slightly in my direction. Can snow blush? I believe I saw the slightest tinge of red blossoming on her cheeks, or was it only the reflection of that red halo of hair she wore? Whichever it was, she immediately lifted her head higher and looked straight ahead, but I saw that now her great green eyes twinkled with something that had not been there before.

I was just wondering if I dared attempt to touch her telepathically, if that were at all possible, when suddenly, without looking at me, she said, 'Why do you stare at me so?'

I was taken unawares. 'Why – because – because you are a fascinating woman. You have strange powers,' I lamely answered.

'And is that all?' Still she stared straight ahead, but I sensed disappointment in her tone.

Encouraged, I told her, 'No, that's not all. You are very beautiful. In my world women are seldom so beautiful.'

'In your world,' she dreamily answered. 'In the Mother-world. And are they also fascinating, these women of the Motherworld?'

'Not like you.'

'Northan would whip you for your boldness. He would have Kota'na set his bears on you.' Her warning was offered in grave tones, but there was colour in her cheeks.

'Is the fervour of Northan's loyalty really so great, or does he lay claim to you as a woman, Armandra?' Having uttered these words I could have bitten my tongue clean through. Her eyebrows lifted and her smile disappeared in a twinkling. She half-lowered her arms and tossed her head angrily, setting her red tresses in motion. Most of her humanity was gone in as much time as it takes to tell. She was now the Woman of the Winds again, a chill priestess of powers unknown.

'Am I a spear or axe or piece of fine fur that a man shall *claim* me?' her voice cracked as sharply as had Northan's whip. 'Northan? He has hopes, the warlord, and he is a strong man and a brave warrior. But a *claim*? No man has any *claim* over Armandra – no man! What mere man could ever hope to hold me, when the winds themselves want me for their bride?'

Finally she turned to me, anger and frustration bubbling up from oceanic depths of eyes, flaming tresses alive upon her head. 'I have promised my people that soon I will take a man, and it will be so. But no man *claims* Armandra. I will have a mate, yes, and bear his children as my duty to the plateau. But he will not be my lover on his terms, nor my "husband" on any terms. His task may give him pleasure but it will only give me children. Children to walk the winds like their mother, and do mortal battle with their unutterable grandfather!'

Now she leaped up – or did she float? – nimbly to the rail of the prow, poising for a moment before diving head-long to breast the air, to spiral up, up to the skies, borne aloft in a cauldron of rushing wind that almost bowled me from my position. She disappeared over the rim of the now looming plateau.

As suddenly as she was gone Northan was at my side. He had plainly been close at hand, had seen the anger in Armandra's face. His own face was not so dark now; blue eyes glittered slyly as he said, 'Perhaps I should have warned you, man of the Motherworld. Men do not speak to Armandra as they do to other women. She is no pretty toy but a princess of the gods.'

He turned as if to leave me, then looked back. 'One other thing; when Armandra takes a mate it will be Northan the Warlord. Others want her, true, and they may challenge my right if they dare. Make sure that *you* do not challenge it. You have yet to pay for shaming me today, in which you were exceedingly lucky and though Armandra has forbidden it I would dearly love to crush you like a snowflake. Do not give me the opportunity.'

'If I loved a woman enough, then I might fight for her, Northan,' I told him. 'But Armandra? She is like the great glacier whose chill wears away even the mountain. Can you warm her, Northan? I doubt it. And take heed; Armandra is no snowflake to be crushed in your hand, and neither am I.'

Now the wind that filled our sails quickly fell away and the twelve ships turned to run parallel with the base of the plateau in single file, gradually slowing upon their polished skis until they were all brought to a halt by use of a system of spiked brakes. Then the great bears were paraded down the gangplanks and chained up in teams fifty strong to haul the snow-ships to anchorage in entrances at the base of the plateau.

As the men and bears finished their various tasks and went off along tunnels that pointed directly into the heart of the vast, flat-topped outcropping, my small party and I began to feel more and more out of things. Ignored and feeling inconsequential, not knowing what else to do, we simply stood idle aboard the snow-ship watching as the members of her crew and their mounts gradually dispersed. Jimmy Franklin tried to catch Kota'na's eye, but the Indian was busy organizing the bears into groups to be led away. Northan had long since gone off with a party of his men.

When it seemed that we were to be left to our own devices, as we descended the steep gangplank to the frozen floor of this rock-walled harbour, a young girl ran out from one of the cavelike entrances to approach us, bowing and curtsying as she came. She was an Indian, and spoke a very broken, pleasantly quaint English.

'She is a Blackfoot!' Jimmy excitedly, laughingly exclaimed. 'A pureblood Blackfoot, not diluted like me through contact with you palefaces.' Then he delighted the girl by speaking in her native tongue. As they conversed, the rest of us kept a polite silence, taking note of how pretty the girl was and the pride of her bearing. She was dressed as richly as an Indian princess, the daughter of a chief, and this opulence was finally explained as Jimmy told us:

'Oontawa is handmaiden and companion to the Woman of the Winds. She has been sent to look after us until we go before the Council of Elders, the "government" of the People of the Plateau. First, though, we are to be shown our quarters. Oontawa will stay with us while we eat. After sleeping, we will see the Council of Elders. They will decide what's to be done with us. Also, there's to be a guided tour of this place. Apparently the plateau is honeycombed with caves and corridors, a multi-level labyrinth like some super beehive!'

'Well, then,' Tracy answered him, 'you'd better tell Oontawa to lead on. I don't know about you boys, but I could do with a bite to eat.'

As we trooped along behind Jimmy Franklin and the Indian girl, with Whitey hobbling along with one arm about Tracy's shoulders and the other around my neck, my sister added, 'Oh, and Jimmy, if I'm going for an interview,' she sniffed disdainfully at the heavy parkas that wrapped her slim girl's figure, 'perhaps Oontawa has a spare fur or two for me? Do be a sweetheart and ask her for me, will you?'

3

In the Hall of the Elders

(Recorded through the Medium of Juanita Alvarez)

After a distance of some forty yards or so, the tunnel we followed into the basalt bowels of the plateau opened into a gallery from which many more tunnels led off. Each of these shafts had its own symbol carved into the rock above it, and Oontawa pointed out the symbol we were to follow to our quarters, a long, inverted heart or arrowhead shape. Once these many symbols were memorized it would not be difficult to find one's way about the cave-system.

The shafts were lighted by flambeaux formed of stone bowls of oil supported upon wooden brackets fixed to the walls at intervals of about fifty feet. The smell of their burning was like a pungent but not overly unpleasant incense. As we went I dipped a finger into one of the bowls, sniffed at the greasy fuel and gingerly tasted it. Mineral oil, with some sweet, sticky additive. I was surprised. Animal fats would have been far more likely. Where would the plateau's people get oil?

On our way we saw single members and groups of the plateau's inhabitants going about their various businesses. They all paid us what passed for compliments as they met us in the corridors. Though they were mainly of Eskimo and Indian extraction, many other elements were also present, including Mongol, white European and white American. Whenever we met up with a group of them they would politely stand aside for us. Oontawa explained that news of my run-in with Northan had already spread and that it had been greeted in many quarters with no uncertain delight. Plainly the warlord's bullying ways were not generally appreciated.

Passing through at least three more galleries and crossing as many major tunnel systems, we finally arrived at a gallery larger than any we had seen so far. Here, cut into the walls between tunnel mouths, rock-hewn steps ascended to higher levels. Climbing a wide stairway and entering a shaft two levels higher, I noted that we seemed to have turned at right angles to our original course, that now we were moving back towards the outer wall of the plateau, which fronted on the white wastes of the frozen plain and the distant scene of the recent battle.

When I mentioned this to Jimmy Franklin, he replied, 'Yes, our apartments are right on the outer wall. Oontawa tells me that we are particularly fortunate; our rooms are comfortable, light and airy, and they command a view overlooking the entire front of the plateau. She says that Tracy's room is really something; all furs and fancy carvings. It seems that Armandra is quite taken with you, Tracy.'

'How much farther are these rooms of ours?' Whitey painfully asked. 'This leg's giving me hell.'

'Almost there,' Jimmy answered.

As he spoke there came the smell of good, hot food from somewhere ahead. Suddenly I was very hungry. 'Jimmy,' I said, 'ask Oontawa what kind of food her people eat, will you? It strikes me that they're bound to be short on vegetables. In fact from what we've seen of this world so far I'd say they only eat meat. But surely they couldn't make out on a diet of meat alone?'

'Sure they could,' he answered. 'The Eskimos of good old Mother Earth have always been meat eaters – *just* meat – and raw at that! In fact that's what the word Eskimo means: "eater of raw meat". And all of the northern Indian tribes lived mainly on meat. They had their berries and fruits, yes, but their diet was ninety per cent flesh, and they did pretty well on it, too.'

Whitey sniffed the air. 'You've convinced me, Jimmy, at least,' he said. 'If that's our meal I can smell – well, I only hope it tastes as good, that's all.'

We rounded a slight bend in the tunnel and natural light suddenly flooded the shaft, showing curtained entrance-ways to caves on both sides. Here, too, the tunnel ended, and we saw that the light came in through square windows cut into the shaft's terminal wall. Oontawa beckoned us forward to these windows, indicating that we should look out.

We were at a height of some seventy feet above the white waste that gently, almost unnoticeably sloped away down to the distant, ominous pyramid whose hazy outline, even at this distance, marred the view. The very sight of the evil altar filled me with the same shuddery feeling I might get from the sight of a black, triangular fin cutting the surface of inviting blue waters . . .

'Rooms with a view,' said Tracy. 'But where's this meal?'

Oontawa led us in through one of the curtained en-trances to a large cave beyond. Since this cave stood away from the outer wall, here the light was from candles in stone holders that stood upon a large ornamental stone table. The weak light of these candles was supplemented by a flickering of flames that leaped up from a metal grille, set in the floor of the farthest corner, to disappear with a quiet, controlled murmur through a similar grille in the ceiling.

While I could feel no change in the temperature (my own flesh remained as chill as Ithaqua's influence had left it), Tracy was obviously delighted with the cave's warmth; she immediately threw off her parkas and stretched her-self luxuriously. 'Hey,' she asked Jimmy, 'do all of these people live like this?'

For in this cave the austerity of the tunnels and passage-ways ended. Here the walls were hung with sumptuous drapes of an American Indian weave; the floors were thick with soft furs; wherever naked rock might have shown unadorned it was carved with ethnic designs so intermingled that their ancient origins were no longer easily discernible.

Oontawa was plainly pleased that we were impressed. She sat down to eat with us. The still steaming meats, of appetizing cuts, were in stone bowls; and I was surprised to note that there were also two types of vegetable prep-arations upon the table, not counting the mushrooms that decorated the central dish, a splendid joint of meat not unlike a leg of pork. Each place of the five at the table was set with a large, slightly hollowed slab of agate and a goblet of the same exotic material.

Jimmy and Oontawa conversed while we ate, but I had little time for talking. I have never enjoyed food so much in my entire life. When at last we were done we washed down the meal with cool sweet water from the goblets. Then Jimmy told us of his conversation with Oontawa.

'I asked her about the fire in the corner there,' he nodded at the flickering column of flame. 'Told her I saw no point in warming the plateau when no one seems to appreciate or need heat. Apparently all of the plateau's outer caves are heated, not for the comfort of their dwellers but simply to stop them from freezing over and filling with ice! Apparently the weather is quite mild at the moment.

'She also tells me that the interiors of all the dwelling-caves are done up in pretty much the same way as this one. She'll show us our personal caves in a moment. I asked her how many people there are in the plateau. She says there are some twenty thousand, and –'

'Twenty thousand!' I cut him off. 'But where did they all come from? They can't be indigenous to Borea?'

Jimmy cocked his head at me. 'They are *now*, I suppose, but certainly their forebears came from Earth, the Motherworld. They were brought here by Ithaqua, just like us. Their history goes back thousands of years, before the races of Earth had writing, but their numbers have been kept down through warring with the Children of the Winds, Ithaqua's own people. It is only recently, since Armandra grew to womanhood, that the People of the Plateau have started to win out over the Wind-Walker's worshippers.

'Now there are twenty thousand of them in the plateau, and room for ten times that number. It is a spare-time task of each family unit or military group to prepare dwelling-caves, barrack halls and stables for future families and armies, future generations. In this way the plateau's many natural tunnel systems have been supplemented over the centuries, or extended and improved. The entire outer wall of the plateau, its face, a fortress, with hundreds of observation posts and hidden exits from which the warriors and their bears can go out to battle in times of siege.'

'Times of siege?' Whitey repeated him. 'You mean when Ithaqua and his lads are about?'

Oontawa nodded, speaking now for herself. 'Yes, when Ithaqua leads Children of Winds against us, then we must stay within walls of plateau or die. Only bravest of our warriors go out to defend outer tunnels and snow-ship harbours.'

'And Armandra?' I asked. 'Does she fight with the warriors, as we saw her fighting today?'

The girl's almond eyes widened and her hand flew to her breast. 'No, lord, not when Ithaqua rides wind, for it is only to trap her and take her back that he wages war against plateau's people. She is his daughter, but she rebels against her father's tyranny, defying him.'

As she finished speaking I saw that my question had disturbed her deeply; the thought of losing Armandra to

102

Ithaqua and the Children of the Winds was too dreadful to contemplate. Now Oontawa stood up.

'Come, I show you your rooms and bathing place. And you –' she turned to Whitey, 'I tend to your leg. Then you all sleep before going to Council of Elders.'

And sleep we did, but not before bathing.

I bathed quickly, along with the other two men, in the hot waters of a cave with a scooped out rock floor. Tracy had a smaller, private bath, a hypocaust affair, in the quite large and sumptuous cave that was her apartment. The water of these baths was constantly changing itself; melting and dripping down from higher, outer ramparts of the plateau, heated by the oil-fire systems of the outer caves and channelled to the baths, finally overflowing to spill away down stone sluices into the plateau's heart, there to turn the wheels of the work-shops.

My own small room was as richly appointed as the others and had a deep square window that looked out over the white wastes. There, stretched out on my back on a pile of furs a foot thick, I quickly fell into a deep, dreamless sleep, one of complete exhaustion and oblivion.

And I came even more quickly awake at the urgent touch of Oontawa's hand. I felt refreshed, reborn, a new man from the moment she shook me awake, and I knew that my sleep must have been a long one.

'Up, up,' Oontawa was saying. 'You are summoned to Council of Elders. Armandra is there. She prepares to see – to see –' She stumbled over her words, searching for an expression. 'She looks over long distances. I do not know, in your tongue, how –'

'Tell me, Oontawa,' said Jimmy Franklin from the door. 'Tell me in your own tongue.'

They conversed rapidly while I put on fur boots, then Jimmy said: 'It appears that Armandra is, well, a seer, I suppose you could call her. She can see things at a distance, with her mind, things that are happening here on

Borea. But she can only do this when – when her father himself is personally concerned.'

Snapping shut the heavy buckle of my fur belt, I turned to Oontawa. 'You mean Ithaqua is back on Borea?'

She nodded. 'He is at his temple. Armandra desires that you should know your enemy better. When she is finished with her seeing, then you speak with Council of Elders. But hurry, they are waiting.'

We went out into the tunnel where Tracy soon joined us. She was dressed in fur trousers, fur boots and a splendid fur jacket with a high collar. She seemed to glow. Whitey appeared last, and it amazed me that his limp was barely noticeable. Whatever ointments these people used, they were certainly effective.

Then, with Oontawa leading, this time following a rock-carved symbol we all recognized well, a five-pointed star! – we proceeded to the Hall of the Elders. The way must have been half a mile, on a course that saw us climbing massive flights of stone stairs and passing through at least a dozen of the great galleries. Finally we approached the end of a wide tunnel that terminated in a smooth stone face of rock through which a great doorway had been cut. Above this entrance a huge five-pointed star was deeply carved in the rock. The Hall of the Elders.

Some fifty feet ahead of us, passing through the entrance in something of a hurry, went three Indians dressed in what looked to me like full ceremonial regalia. Jimmy stared after them and gasped. 'Blackfoot, Chinook and Nootka, chiefs of the most northerly of the Northwest Tribes, just as they were two hundred years ago! Ithaqua doesn't seem to have strayed off limits very far south of the Canadian border.'

'Come,' Oontawa whispered, leading the way through the door. 'We are last to enter, but not too late.'

We followed her into a vast cave or chamber lit by huge, brightly flaring flambeaux. The first thing that caught my eye was a carved throne in the dead centre of the chamber. Decked in furs and standing upon a raised section of the floor with stone steps leading up to it, the thing was massively ornate. Seated upon it with her white hands curved over its stone arms, her head upright and her eyes closed, was Armandra. Her breast moved slowly beneath the beautiful jacket of fox fur that she wore.

She was in a deep trancelike state; before her face, hanging motionless from a golden chain suspended from the top of the high throne's back where it curved forward over her head, was the medallion she had previously worn about her neck. Motionless? Perhaps not. The medallion was not distinct to my eyes; its disc seemed blurred. Slowly, very slowly, it turned on its golden chain.

The second most noticeable thing in the Hall of the Elders was the silence. Though the descending tiers of stone benches that circled the amphitheatre-like chamber were filled almost to capacity, not a single whisper stirred the assembly. Or was I mistaken in this also? Mistaken I was, for now I heard a distinct sound, a humming as of winds blowing far away, and it issued from that slowly turning, *vibrating* medallion!

The medallion hummed and vibrated, echoing however faintly the hum and roar of weird winds blowing out beyond the rim of the universe. It hung before Armandra's face and she heard it, and I knew instinctively that its voice formed pictures for her – sounds transmuted into visions – so that what she heard she also saw.

But now Oontawa was standing on tiptoe, whispering something urgently into my ear and tugging at my hand, indicating that my party should take seats. A space had been cleared for us; the occupants of the lowest tiers of seats had moved silently along to make room. I blinked my eyes and shook my head. I had been very nearly hypnotized by the sight of Armandra in her trance.

105

As I followed Tracy and my friends to our places, every eye in the Hall of the Elders was upon me. At a guess some four thousand eyes frowned at me, the latecomer. While we sat down Oontawa moved quickly to the raised dais, climbing its steps to stand at the left hand of Armandra. For a moment she leaned forward to peer anxiously into Armandra's white face, at the closed eyes and drawn, regal features. Then she kneeled and bowed her head, this handmaiden to a goddess.

The silence in the Hall of the Elders seemed to deepen, or perhaps it was simply that the humming and roaring of the suspended medallion increased. Whichever, soon it was as though a torrent of whispering ghost-winds rushed through the chamber. And ghost-winds they must have been, for despite the fact that the distant tumult rapidly increased, not a single breath of disturbed air touched us and the fires of the flambeaux burned as steadily as before. And now I sensed that the rushing of air was only an illusion, like the crash of waves heard in a shell, an illusion magnified by the absolute silence of the assembly.

So the shock of Armandra's voice, clear, golden and bell-like, breaking that ghost-ridden whisper of weird winds, was electric! I felt the hair of my neck prickle as she spoke, and instantly all heads turned once more in the direction of my party. The Woman of the Winds was speaking in English, plainly for our benefit, and in the eyes of all present our importance had immediately trebled.

'Ithaqua stands atop his altar,' Armandra intoned in a voice which, except for its singular golden ring, was so void of modulation or emotion that it might have been the voice of Death himself. 'He is returned from dark meditations in the moons of Borea and now awaits his tribute – of which there is none, for we have snatched the girl he lusted after and the men whose souls he wanted from the very jaws of his wolf-warriors!

106

'There he stands.' Her hand, alabaster in motion, trembling slightly, pointed eerily across the hall at nothing. Her eyes remained closed; her hair, living fire, stirred strangely and began to rise up over her head. 'There he stands atop his pedestal of ice, my *father*!' The last word fell like a golden icicle from her lips, seeming to splinter into shards of ice in the air of the great cave.

Her hand fell back to rest upon the carved arm of her throne while her hair continued its coppery swirling above her head. 'They gather, his priests, cowering about the foot of his altar: whipped wolf puppies that snarl at each other, eager to give the blame, grovelling within the circle of totems. Outside the totem ring the Children of the Winds wait. Ithaqua has called them forth from far across the white wastes to see his justice. And he *is* just, for he commanded and his commands went unanswered, his hunger unappeased. And how shall a god correct such deliberate contempt?

'But see, there are only six of them within the totem ring. The High Priest is not there . . .

'Ah, *now* I see him!' She leaned forward slightly, her fingers tightening upon the arms of her throne. 'I see the dog, fighting and screaming, dragged from his hiding place and thrown before the altar of his master. He grovels, begs, pleads – this so-called priest who dared to threaten, to curse me – and Ithaqua stands over him, dark atop the pyramid of ice. Now the groveller rages at the lesser priests and they cower, fearing the Wind-Walker's wrath. But the Wind-Walker is cold and still.

'Now the High Priest bows himself down, kneels and cries out his innocence to Ithaqua, giving the six lesser priests the blame. Ah, but they stand united now, those six, ringing him about and pointing their accusation.

'See! The game is up! He tries to run! . . . They bring him down! . . . And now – *now Ithaqua takes a hand!*'

It became obvious to me then that the entire audience understood at least the rudiments of the English language; almost every head in that great cave, my own included, must have moved forward in unison as Armandra spoke those words. I sensed the concerted movement all about me; the rapt attention of every one of us was full upon Armandra. And we all saw and gasped together at the change that stole swiftly over her face.

A ruddy light seemed to burn upon her cheeks, upon her high brow and closed eyes, subtly complementing the flaming copper of her hair. The medallion upon its chain glittered brightly as its gyrations grew more visibly erratic, its humming and roaring forming a definite presence in the great chamber.

Armandra leaned forward further yet until her face almost touched the spinning disc. Her fingers gripped the arms of her throne like claws. Gone now was the calm, deathlike mask she had worn. In its place a feral skull snarled beneath wildly swaying masses of burning hair.

This was the moment I had waited for, my chance to attempt a penetration of Armandra's mind. Oh, I entertained no real doubt that her trance was genuine – nor did I doubt that she was indeed the daughter of Ithaqua – but if the latter were true then she was only half human, spawn of a demon or god of the Cthulhu Cycle of Myth, in which event I should at least be able to gauge the power and direction of her mental emissions.

As to *why* I wanted to do this thing: I found in this woman-creature a vast enigma, a great challenge. Not once did I think of myself as an intruder. If her concentration was as great as it appeared to be, then she would not even notice my presence. When I think now of my audacity . . .

Tentatively I reached out my mind to her, and instantly I was *enveloped*!

She was a whirlpool of concentrated mental energy that sucked me in like a spider flushed down a drain. I could neither fight nor withdraw. I became part of her, hearing what she heard, seeing what she saw. And so superior was her power that my own puny energies were not even perceptible in the mental vortex.

Physically I sat there on that stone bench between Tracy and Jimmy Franklin, but mentally I was a mote in the cosmos of Armandra's psyche. I whirled away with her on the wings of strange winds and stared down with her upon a distant scene . . .

4

'Bring this Man to Me!'

(Recorded through the Medium of Juanita Alvarez)

'*Now Ithaqua takes a hand!*'

The words seemed to repeat over and over, receding into vast distances and returning to reverberate in my mind. Then abruptly, there was only the wind; a wind that blew mournfully across the white wastes, bringing with it the distant howling of frightened wolves. And perhaps those wolves sensed that which would frighten any living creature: Ithaqua, the Thing that Walks on the Wind!

For now I saw him, bloated with anger where he stood at the apex of his pyramid altar, and I saw the six priests scatter like cockroaches as the monster stepped down onto the frozen surface within the totem ring. Ah, but those were no human feet with which the Wind-Walker strode the crushed snow. They were huge and webbed, out of all proportion even to the towering size he had attained, which now lifted him head and shoulders above his own altar.

Doomed, Zchakow the Russian fled, feet flying, arms reaching, eyes bulging and fear foaming from between his champing jaws. He fled before the tread of his monstrous master.

With a thrill of pure horror I suddenly found myself lusting for the Russian's blood, eager to see him struck down and destroyed! It dawned on me that this was not Hank Silberhutte but Armandra. I was now part of Armandra, influenced by her emotions, her desires, which were stronger than mine. And yet, paradoxically, human compassion was not absent in her; indeed it was strong. I could feel it like the pulse of a powerful heart. Ah, but that compassion was fighting a losing battle with her inhuman side, the incalculably alien and abhorrent cruelty inherited from her father. And Zchakow was her enemy.

Now I moved closer to the terrible drama being enacted down on the frozen plain. Out between the carved totems raced Boris Zchakow, his face twisted with hideous fear. He was, or had been, Ithaqua's High Priest, with power of life and death over the Children of the Winds. He *knew* his master; he recognized his fate. And perhaps it was this knowledge of that ultimate fate of all of Ithaqua's followers that robbed the Russian of his senses. When I saw what that fate was, I thought that I too might easily go mad confronted with it.

But even transfixed with horror, feeling empathy with the madman with every psychic nerve I possessed, nevertheless I also thrilled to the chase. For Armandra was Hank Silberhutte, and he was only a tiny part of Armandra, and both were lost now to a raging vortex of bloodlust!

I remembered her face as I had last seen it: a skull-like mask surmounted by living, flaming hair; lips drawn back from gleaming white teeth; the whole burning with hell's own fires. And now I saw that face again, only her eyes were no longer closed.

Carmine pits blazed where only depths of submarine green had opened before, eyes that burned with the energies of alien suns, and somewhere, like subdued background music to a conversation, I heard again a concerted gasping from two thousand throats.

The Hall of the Elders! Struggling still to free myself from Armandra's magnet mind, I had almost made it back to that great cave deep in the bowels of the plateau, only to be snatched back again to my mental vantage point above the Temple of Ithaqua.

111

In that same instant, as if my mind were not already more than sufficiently whirling, I sensed that something was different, wrong – terribly wrong! I was no longer merely a part of the Woman of the Winds but of something far greater, something utterly alien.

Ithaqua-Armandra – I brushed aside massive totems, smashing them like matchsticks, reached to snatch the gibbering lunatic from the frozen ground and hold him high aloft. He – we tossed him into the sky, limbs thrashing like a crippled bird, catching him before he could crash to earth.

Then we laughed, Ithaqua-Armandra and I – laughed in a maelstrom of mirth that I knew could only be subdued, could only end in an act of the cruellest horror.

I fought against the unholy glee that filled me, fought to be free of its hold as it moved toward livid, lunatic rage. But I might as well have tried to beat down the winds with my bare fists. And Armandra fought too, bravely, but uselessly, as the human side of her nature strove harder than ever to turn her back from her monstrous sire's dread attraction.

Physically I was Hank Silberhutte, a man sitting between his sister and a friend in the Hall of the Elders; mentally I was a telepathic observer, an unseen intruder, a part of Armandra's psyche. But since she in turn had been drawn into the Ithaqua id, then I was also part of Him. Part of the ultimate horror. He had planned for Boris Zchakow.

The Wind-Walker, Armandra and I stared through avid carmine orbs, shrinking ocean depths of green, flinching blue slits, as he-she-we lifted Zchakow up to his-her-my face, where he screamed and frothed as Ithaqua-Armandra-I scrutinized him minutely.

Then, in another instant, it was over. We threw back our hideous head and lifted the shrieking figure of the mad, wildly kicking Russian up, up into the air. A sudden moan of horror, rising to rival the mournfully moaning wind, came up from the assembled thousands of Ithaqua's people, held captive audience. But no, they could not watch, they had seen this before. To a man they turned and fled, even those six lesser priests whose accusations had brought Zchakow to this – to the very gates of hell! Yes, the gates of hell, in the shape of Ithaqua's eyes – *into one of which he-she-I now dropped the wriggling form of the mad Russian!*

A bubbling scream, shrill and rising, cut off in a shower of carmine sparks that burst upwards from the flickering rim of that seething crater eye like lava bombs from a volcano – and Zchakow was gone.

And I had felt something. Something which I cannot, *must* not attempt to describe in detail, except to say that perhaps it was an overflow of Ithaqua's hideous *satisfaction* . . .

Now for a moment the Wind-Walker grimly surveyed the fleeing hordes of his people, then turned to stride up a staircase of air back to his position at the summit of the pyramid altar. There he stood, arms akimbo, great feet gripping the sides of the ice mountain, and as his rage subsided I found myself freed of the tremendous attraction of his id. I began to withdraw, to retreat along with Armandra from the mental maw of the Wind-Walker.

– And at that very moment he saw us!

No, he saw *her*, only Armandra, for my own feeble essence was insignificant. I call it essence because I realize now that it was no simple mind-web that had enmeshed me, and therefore that I had not been trapped telepathically. After all, I had looked into Ithaqua's mind before without any of this. But the power Armandra had which enabled her to visit and observe scenes afar was more than merely telepathic; it was more truly psychic, the essential power of the id itself. Her *Ka* had been part of her awesome father for a few brief moments of time, hers

113

and mine too; and now, when we had almost managed to break free –

Quickly the scene of the monster atop his pyramid of ice shrank as I fled with Armandra back toward the plateau, and quickly Ithaqua turned his head to stare after us, realization growing in the flickering of his flaring eyes. He reached out bestial psychic arms after Armandra, again casting that net whose meshes she had managed to escape before he even knew she was there. Ah, but now he *did* know she was there, and again she was caught.

Armandra was caught and so was I, and it seemed as good a time as any to make my presence known, this time telepathically, as I had intended in the first place.

'*Armandra!*' I cried with my mind. '*Fight him. You have to fight him. I'm here to help you. Together we can beat him!*'

'*What?*' Armandra's mind reached out unbelievingly to mine. '*Who is it that offers aid, and how did –*' but that was all.

At last Ithaqua had seen me too, but too late. Something that seethed like acid touched my mind, touched Armandra, too, then burned through to the Being of Ithaqua himself. He staggered atop his pyramid. He snatched back those greedily reaching mental and physical arms of his and slammed down the shutters of his alien id, his psyche, his mind, cutting us free of him. No, cutting *himself* free of us! We fled back to our bodies in the Hall of the Elders.

I was stretched out full length on the stone floor. Tracy and Jimmy were trying to get me to my feet. I shook my head and stood up, noting that the chamber was now empty of all but a group of magnificently robed old men, my own party, Oontawa, and –

I started forward when I saw Armandra being helped down the dais steps to Oontawa. The Indian girl's eyes flashed a warning, saying that this was not the time to approach the Woman of the Winds. But perhaps she was wrong.

Armandra's beautiful face was drawn, strained. As she passed close to me she held up a trembling hand and turned my way. 'What is your name, man of the Motherworld?'

'Hank,' I told her. 'Hank Silberhutte.'

'And it was you that –?'

I nodded. 'Yes.'

She leaned toward me, searching my face. 'At the end there – what was it that came to sting my mind, burning Ithaqua and making him release me?'

'Was it this?' Tracy asked, holding up one of the five-pointed star-stones from her neck, where the fur of her jacket had kept it and its twin hidden. 'When you cried out, Hank, when you shouted to Armandra that she must fight her father, I sort of instinctively held the stone up before your eyes. Then you leaped up and fell to the floor, and Armandra almost toppled from her throne.'

Tracy stopped talking, gazed nervously about as the elders all around her stepped quickly back, away from the star-stone sigil, and I stepped back with them. Armandra's eyes grew huge and round. She pointed a trembling hand at the powerful symbol of old gods spinning at the end of the chain Tracy held. Then she fell back weakly, leaning on Oontawa.

The group of elders, ten of them, now clustered closer, and one of them stretched out a finger before I could offer a warning. Briefly he touched the star-stone – and instantly snatched his finger back, the skin of its tip scorched and blackened. For a moment anguish showed on his face, then he turned to his colleagues.

'The stone is genuine – and yet,' he stared fascinated at Tracy, 'the girl is unhurt!'

'Elders, I go now,' Armandra broke in, stronger now, commanding everyone's attention. 'But there are things I would know. See to the strangers and ask what questions you will, but do not keep these people here too long. They are to be our special guests until I decide on the best way to employ their talents.' She turned to move on, paused.

'This man,' she barely looked at me, 'Oontawa will return for him. She will bring him to me.' With that she turned and walked with her handmaiden from the hall.

When the two had gone, the oldest of the ten elders invited us to talk. He was an Eskimo of very ancient lineage, a tough old ivory chief of tribes forgotten except in Arctic legend. Explaining that his English was very, very bad, he spoke through Jimmy Franklin, turning his attention immediately to Tracy.

I had noticed that the elders seated themselves carefully out of her way for an obvious reason. Now, to explain her immunity to the star-stones whose shape was the greatest symbol of benign power known to the People of the Plateau. Despite their perfectly natural dread of the real item, it was necessary that we tell our entire story right from the beginning. This we did, using Jimmy as our interpreter whenever we were in difficulties.

The elders were fascinated with our story, astounded that we had deliberately set out to track Ithaqua down, and when our tale was done they stood up to give us their applause. Then their youngest member, a man until now silent, finally said, 'Permit me to introduce myself. I am Charlie Tacomah, a Shawnee late of the Motherworld.'

'A Shawnee who speaks perfect English,' Jimmy answered him, eyeing the tall, bronzed figure whose features, though fine, were plainly American Indian. 'But Nashville and Chattanooga are a long way from the Arctic Circle, and you are a much younger man than the others here.'

'I think he's a man pretty much like yourself, Jimmy,' Whitey said. 'A man of the reservations, who figured that there might be better things in life. I guess his ambitions led him astray, though.'

The elder nodded, glancing at Whitey appreciatively. 'Yes, it was twenty-eight years ago. After the war when I got back home to Memphis, I found the same old prejudices. I wanted to do something about it, decided to write a book on all the Indian tribes, ancient and modern. I eventually travelled north, seeking out the little-known Eskimo tribes, and –'

'We can guess,' I broke in on him sympathetically. 'You fell afoul of Ithaqua. He brought you to Borea.'

Charlie Tacomah nodded. 'I lived for a few days with the Children of the Winds, then ran off and came here. The elders found out that I was something of a military strategist – I had been a major in the infantry – and I became adviser to the old warlords. Five years ago Northan took over as warlord, controlling all of the plateau's army, and I was granted a seat in the Council of Elders.

'Of all the People of the Plateau, I reckon that about sixty of them have arrived here on Borea within the last twenty or thirty years. They learn to fit in pretty quickly. Of course, the great majority of folks that Ithaqua brings stay out on the plains, too frightened to try to escape. If an escapee is recaptured,' he shrugged, 'Ithaqua has his own ways of punishing deserters.'

'And now?' Tracy prompted him after a moment's silence. 'What's to become of us?'

'Well, you heard what Armandra said. There's not a great deal we can do with you just yet. Right now, though, it is my pleasure to show you all around the plateau; a fascinating place, as you'll see. Eventually my colleagues' proposals will be put before Armandra for her approval. It is not anticipated that you will be required to contribute in any mundane fashion to the plateau's welfare. Of course, you are far different from run-of-the-mill newcomers.'

As he finished speaking Oontawa returned. Tracy cocked her head to one side and smiled wickedly at me. She whispered: 'Here comes the handmaiden, Hank. Before she takes you to Armandra, you'd better promise me you'll be a good boy. I've noticed the way you look at the Woman of the Winds.'

'Star-stones or not,' I told her, grinning, 'another crack like that, little sister, and you go over my knee – and I'll do a bit of wind-raising myself!'

And so I started out with Oontawa for Armandra's apartments, and it immediately became apparent that the Priestess of the Plateau dwelt in the topmost levels of her realm. Staircase after stone staircase we climbed, ever spiralling upward through basalt caverns and tunnels until I was sure we must soon reach the battlements of the roof; and we could not have been far short of that roof when finally we came to the first corridor I had seen with its own selected guardsmen.

During our long climb the symbols above tunnel entrances or at the feet of the staircases had been gradually narrowing down to a handful, but already I had guessed which symbol led to Armandra: that of a flash of lightning. Sure enough, above that last, guarded corridor entrance, the lightning flash was the sole remaining symbol, and I saw that beyond it even the tunnel walls themselves were draped with priceless furs.

Two huge squat Eskimo guards, each attended by a towering white bear that swayed and yawned in a rock-cut niche to his rear, stood up straight and saluted with their viciously barbed, ceremonial harpoons as we passed. Flambeaux were now absent where natural light flooded in through windows lining the vast curve of the outer wall. By 'windows' I may give the wrong impression; I paused to look out through one of them and found myself staring into a shaft, for the window was cut through a wall of rock all of fifteen feet thick!

Closer to our destination the light flooded in more brightly, and here I saw that the thickness of the outer wall was much diminished. We came to a huge, iron-barred balcony with a stone ceiling; the balcony reached out from the face of the plateau into open air. Now I saw indeed that we were at a great height above the white waste. Fighting the wind that howled in from outside, I put my head out between the bars and looked down. More than two hundred and fifty feet beneath me, the rocky base of the plateau froze into the surface of the surrounding ground. Craning my neck I looked upward and saw that the topmost ramparts were still some twenty to thirty feet higher than this level, that the solid rock above my head must form the ceiling of Armandra's rooms.

I turned to Oontawa, saying: 'A dangerous place. A careless person could be sucked out by the wind, or fall through the bars.'

She nodded. 'Yes, Armandra sometimes – walks out – from here. When she seeks solitude.'

With those innocent words, so naively spoken, the Indian girl brought back to me all that I had tried to forget of the woman who was about to give me audience. Here was I, going to Armandra's apartments almost like some fancy courtier on his way to the boudoir of a precocious princess, and yet it was not like that at all. Armandra was more goddess than woman, as much an alien creature as a human being, and I was merely a man of the Motherworld.

Oontawa chattered away as we walked the perimeter corridor, practising her English and doubtlessly trying to be very informative, but I scarcely heard a word she said; my mind was now fully on her mistress. Perhaps fifty yards beyond the great balcony we came to a curtained entrance where the lightning flash symbol was inlaid in gold: the door to Armandra's quarters. Oontawa passed through the curtains ahead of me, murmuring something as she went, but again my mind was not on what the Indian girl was saying. I followed directly behind her through the curtains.

The room beyond was gorgeously appointed, rich as an eastern sultan's wildest dreams of opulence. Delicately carved, curtained archways led off into adjoining rooms; soft furs of a texture and colouring guaranteed to delight any furrier of the Motherworld overlapped across the floor; the white walls were carved with pillars and arches and intricate arabesques; gold and silver ornaments stood in arched niches in the walls, and fretted agate and marble furniture was cushioned with white furs as soft as freshly fallen snow. But in the very centre of the room stood the greatest wonder of all – Armandra, rising naked from a crystal pool!

We saw each other and froze, and simultaneously Oontawa realized that I had followed her into the chamber of her mistress without waiting. She turned with a sharp cry of consternation, her almond eyes wide and flashing.

'Calm yourself, Oontawa,' Armandra said. 'I am sure that my guest has seen naked women before. The Motherworld is full of "fascinating" women!'

Stepping from the pool she folded herself in a white fur wrap that covered her body completely. Before her feet vanished in the robe's folds, I thought for a moment that I saw something odd about them. What it was I could not have said exactly, just that they seemed to be – scarred? It had been only a glimpse.

'Well,' she continued, shaking her red hair and sprinkling crystal droplets all about, 'you might as well sit, Hank Silberhutte, or do all men of the Motherworld stand like statues with their mouths open?'

At that I offered an awkward, embarrassed grin, in answer to which I saw mischievous lights dancing momentarily in the depths of her fjord eyes. 'Oontawa, leave us,' she told the girl. 'I will call you when I want you. Oh! –' she called out in an afterthought as, with a look of disbelief stamped upon her face, the girl turned to go. 'Though I trust you above all others, Oontawa, make sure you say

120

nothing of this man's unfortunate eagerness to attend me; there are those it would surely enrage. You may see to it that the elders, too, remain silent about this interview. Particularly those with whom the warlord has influence.'

Oontawa bowed and went out through the curtains. I sat at a delicately carved table, hardly daring to rest the weight of my arms upon it in case it fell apart. Armandra seated herself upon the fur cushions of a settee carved of a single gigantic agate, hugging her robe about her and gazing at me curiously.

She said: 'Are your hands gentle, Hank Silberhutte?'

Again she had me tongue-tied. 'My hands?'

'Are they *gentle*,' she frowned impatiently, 'for the drying of my hair?'

'They can be gentle,' I answered, 'when they need to be.'

'Good. Come and dry my hair.'

I went to her and took the square of woven material that she handed me. She continued: 'I know that your hands can be hard, for you knocked down that strutting bear, Northan. But I expect that they are soft, too; how else would you handle all of those "fascinating" women of the Motherworld?'

I caught up her damp tresses and began to dry them, pausing to turn her head away so that I could make a decent job of it.

'Your hands *are* gentle,' she told me, laughing at me out of sea green eyes. 'Perhaps I'll find a place for you as a handmaiden, and –'

At that point I stopped her. To say what she had said to any man, which most ordinary women of Earth would know better than to do, would surely be folly. To say it to a Texan . . .

I turned her head back and kissed her fiercely, feeling her fingers fly to the back of my neck and head to tear at my hair, ignoring the shock and anger obvious in her suddenly squirming, furiously fighting body, until she no longer fought but sank her nails into my neck and drank as deeply as I.

For a moment only!

Then, as I relaxed my hold upon her, she snatched herself back from me and slapped me so hard that my ears rang.

'You beautiful *witch*!' I said through clenched teeth.

But now she tilted her head warningly and I thought her eyes were suddenly flecked with pink. Those great eyes widened and, seemingly of its own accord, the still damp hair of her head lifted eerily to float free of her shoulders. For a moment she was a goddess again, utterly inhuman. But then, amazingly, she burst into tears and buried her face in her hands!

5

Armandra Chooses a Mate

(Recorded through the Medium of Juanita Alvarez)

Her tears were the perfectly normal tears of a woman face to face with utter mental and physical frustration. The tears of a *woman*, not a being of supermundane powers. Telepathically probing the edge of her emotions, gently, so as to remain undiscovered, I found a stark island of bitter frustration afloat in a sea of loneliness.

Whitey's words came back to me, about Ithaqua's need for a companion: *It's a terribly lonely existence*, he had said, *walking the spaces between the spheres*. How much more true for a human or half-human child of the Snow Thing with alien powers trapped in a human psyche, framed by human emotions?

Carefully, concentrating on what I was doing, I allowed sympathy to flow along the line of one-way communication I had established, and instantly the bleak hopelessness in Armandra's mind began to soften. She lifted her head and leaned toward me, searching my face with eyes as round as saucers. Her tears were already drying.

'Was it really you, Hank, that came to me when my father held me fast?'

I nodded, answering her in a manner guaranteed to satisfy her curiosity and quell any last doubt she might have. 'Yes.' I said. '*It really was. It's a power I have.*'

And she could see that it was so, that I was speaking in her mind. Proof of my success showed in her frown, then in the widening of eyes already huge. 'A very dangerous power,' she said, forming her words carefully. 'How can any woman trust a man who listens to her thoughts?'

'She must first learn to believe that he would not listen uninvited,' I answered. Then I launched into an explanation of my telepathic power, briefly telling her what I had already made known to the Council of Elders. 'So you see,' I finished, 'that among my colleagues of the Motherworld it is considered outrageous for one telepath to "listen" to another without his permission. But in any case, my own power is rather special.'

And there I paused, for how could I say that I was limited to intercourse with alien thoughts, the hideous mental gibberings of monsters, when Armandra herself was now a vehicle for my talent? I groped for words. 'I can only detect the thoughts of – of very special Beings.'

'Other people?'

'There is one other woman I can talk to in this fashion,' I hedged, 'and she is like a sister, the same as Tracy.'

'But you have listened to my mind. Is it not so?'

'No, not really. When you spied upon your father out over the frozen wastes, it was not telepathy that trapped me there when you were trapped. It was your own power, yours and your father's, a power in no way like mine. It is far greater, different.'

She nodded, warming to the empathy growing between us. 'I believe you. I know it is true. The power I have, which came to me from my father, is not like yours. But have you not listened to my mind within the last few moments, here in this very room?'

'No,' I again denied it. 'I merely felt your hurt, your loneliness, and tried to comfort you. I have not stolen a single thought out of your lovely head, though any man might easily be tempted to try. Particularly if he thought you were thinking about him.' I stared at her pointedly.

'One day, Hank Silberhutte, I might invite you into my head,' she said, quite seriously. 'Would you come to me if I called you? If I needed you?'

'That I promise.'

'But wait,' she said. 'I have heard *your* voice talking to *my* mind, yes, but how do we know if –'

'Would you like to try an experiment?'

She nodded eagerly.

'Then think something at me, anything. See if I can read it in your mind.'

She opened her eyes wide and stared straight at me. It was very strange, that sensation, like the chiming of golden bells at the bottom of some mental well, rising slowly to the surface, forming pictures. I looked, then chuckled as the mischievous lights again lit in Armandra's eyes. 'Yes,' I nodded, 'I think perhaps Northan would be angry if he knew I was here. But it does not worry me. Do you fear him, Armandra?'

'Fear Northan? I fear only Ithaqua – but I know that many of my people, even a handful of the elders, do fear the warlord.' Her eyes narrowed thoughtfully. 'He is ambitious. And he does not like his ambitions thwarted. You must watch out for him, Hank. Be very watchful of Northan.'

'It surprises me,' I said, 'that he was not in the Hall of the Elders for your – seeing.'

'No, he would be celebrating the victory of the ships over the wolf-warriors. Sometimes the celebrations last for days. Oh, they strut and boast, as their forefathers did before them. In many ways they are like children.'

'Well,' I answered, 'the battle was well won, with your help. But without you Northan would have been hard put. And he lost a lot of face when I returned his blows. I can hardly see that he has much to celebrate!'

'Oh, he'll knock a few heads together, find excuses for your beating him on his own ship and awe his cronies with feats of strength.' Again her eyes narrowed. 'I know Northan the Warlord. It will not take him long to regain whatever face he feels he has lost. He is ambitious.' Again that word.

'And what is his ambition, do you think?'

'Is it not obvious?' she lifted her eyebrows. 'He desires to share these apartments with me. For while the People of the Plateau are satisfied with their princess, Northan would give them a king, a High Priest. And in a way the elders aid him, for they want me to have children.'

'But you do not want him?'

'I could do worse,' she tossed her hair, dry now, and began to comb it. 'Does the thought annoy you?'

'No,' I immediately answered, then bit my tongue and spoke in her mind. '*You damn well know it does!*'

She laughed. 'Because I am fascinating, and beautiful?'

'Those are good reasons,' I agreed.

'I am not all beautiful,' she told me, her face becoming serious in an instant. 'You saw my feet when I left the pool?'

'Your feet? Yes, they looked –'

She flicked the fur wrap so that it flew wide below her knees. 'They are ugly!' she said.

For a moment she stared down in something like horror at her feet, then said: 'My mother was stolen from your green Earth by Ithaqua. She was given into the care of the Children of the Winds until I was born. Later, in my father's absence, having learned that he had fathered a child upon a human woman, the plateau people stole me away in a raid and brought me here; my mother too, but she died from the wound of a harpoon hurled in the fighting. They say she was very beautiful.

'The elders raised me. When I was ten a physician, specially trained for ten years to perform one work, cut my feet down from the great webbed pads they were to their present shape. He was supposed to leave them looking like normal human feet, so that I would forget my origins, but the operation was not very successful. For a long time I was in constant pain.'

A moment longer I looked at her feet. They were the shape of human feet but with square looking, nailless toes and a covering of smooth scar tissue. Then she flicked her wrap back into place.

'When my feet had healed, about a year after the operation, I had a terrible dream of great angry winds and of the physician whose knives had scarred me. When I awakened the elders told me that there had been an accident; that same physician had fallen from a window of his room high in the outer wall of the plateau. A freak gust of wind, they said.

'When I told them that I had sent that wind to kill him – sent it in my sleep to settle a debt I hardly recognized in my waking hours – then they stood in awe of me and knew that they could never suppress that in me which was of Ithaqua. Thus I became what I am.

'But there,' she looked at me and sighed. 'Now you must go. Soon I meet with the elders again and I need a few hours sleep. The seeing drained me. Today was especially hard. I became too involved with my father's awful justice. He has never come so close to trapping me before. But, Hank Silberhutte, I am glad you are my friend. And I know that if I call you will come to me. Now go.'

'There's a lot you could tell me, many questions you –'

'Your questions will be answered, in time.' She stood up, holding her wrap about her. She held out her free hand and I took it, following her to the curtained exit. 'Only promise me,' she said, 'that however tempted you may be, you will never look into my mind uninvited. When I want you to know my thoughts, you shall know them.'

'I promise.'

'Wait!' she cried as I was about to leave. 'You gave me something I did not ask for. Now take it back.' She leaned forward, brushed my lips with hers, and quickly withdrew. Seeing the mischief rising in her eyes I reached out my arms to her, and she drew the curtains in my face and was gone.

On returning to my room I felt suddenly exhausted. That experience I had shared with Armandra's psyche had severely sapped my strength, as much as the fight against her father's alien will had taxed hers. Since the others were not back yet from their sightseeing, I lay down and slept.

No sooner had I awakened than they returned. They were tired, but so full of what they had seen I decided that in the near future I must explore the plateau for myself.

'This place,' said Whitey, 'is a maze of marvels. We've seen the wells that supply half of the plateau's water, and the cavern where weeds and mushrooms grow at the edge of the geyser flats. We've seen cave pools chock-full of fish, and watched the Eskimos spearing them.'

'From the other side of the plateau,' Tracy cut in, 'we've seen the rim of Borea's sun. Like the moons, it never moves; only its upper curve shows. There's a forest of pines on that side, too, and in the distance a great stretch of woodland that reaches to the horizon. It looks like a rather flat version of Canada.'

Jimmy was less enthusiastic. 'We saw the pool of oil where they draw their fuel in wooden buckets, and we saw the dark tunnel whose entrance has a skull carved above it as a warning. We felt the horror lurking there, emanating from forbidden nether-caves. No one knows what lies at the tunnel's lower level; its mysteries have never been explored. It reeks of – fear!'

When Tracy shivered I knew it was not because of any normal chill she might feel. 'It's funny,' she said. 'Jimmy and Whitey felt this – this *thing* – and so did Charlie Tacomah. All of the People of the Plateau feel it when they are close to the tunnel. No one will enter it, not by a single step. And yet I felt nothing. Well, I felt something, but not fear. If anything, I felt safer there. But not really safe, if you know what I mean.' Suddenly she clung to my arm: 'Hank, when can we . . . I mean, do you think –'

'Tracy,' Whitey cut her off. 'Let's have it out in the open. We must all have thought of the same thing, and I've been trying my best to see what the outcome might be. You know, I've been looking for a hunch. But I haven't found one.'

'You don't come over too well, Whitey,' I told him. 'You mean we're stuck here?'

He nodded. 'I think so. It looks like we're here for good. If these people have been on Borea for thousands of years and haven't found a way back yet, what chance do we stand?'

Tracy looked miserable so I put my arm round her. 'Not much of a chance,' I agreed. Then I thought of Armandra and realized that the thought of staying on Borea hadn't really been bothering me too much.

'Still,' I added, 'never say die.'

For me the next month passed slowly. I seemed always to be waiting for a call from Armandra, but I only saw her twice, at meetings of the council to which I was invited as a courtesy. On both occasions, though, I had caught her eyes on me when she thought I was looking elsewhere. Between times my dreams were full of her.

Once I dreamed we walked together on the wind between the worlds. We moved where stars were frosted to the firmament and Borea was far away. And yet, though I saw Armandra mostly in my dreams, there was always this peculiar feeling that she was with me in the waking world also. I began to suspect that she was 'peeking' into my mind. If so then she knew well enough by now my feelings for her.

I say the time passed slowly, and yet there were diversions. The plateau's weapon-masters took me in hand and I was trained for three hours daily in a variety of weapons. I soon discovered that what skill could not achieve in a tight spot might often be realized by use of my considerable size and strength. And my strength never failed to amaze my instructors.

During one such session Northan entered the exercise cave. I was throwing a harpoon at a painted target of woven hide when the warlord came in. I saw him and his presence put me off; my throw went a few inches wide of the bull.

Northan grinned and picked up a harpoon. 'Not nearly good enough,' he said. 'If that target was a wolf, he'd be tearing you in half by now.'

He turned, casually hurled his weapon and it slammed home dead centre of the target, burying its barbs. We moved to the target together. 'Now that was a cast,' Northan chuckled.

He tugged at the shaft of his harpoon but it was stuck fast. Lifting a foot to the target, he strained. Still the harpoon would not come. He grunted, shrugged, stepped back. I caught hold of both weapons, one in each hand, placed a knee against the target and pulled the harpoons free in a snapping of leather thongs. Northan's face went grey, then darkened over. Before he could speak I said, 'That wolf you mentioned might not find me such easy meat, Northan. Perhaps, seeing you weaponless, he'd turn on you instead.'

It was just a small incident, but word of this second encounter spread as rapidly as the story of our confrontation on the snow-ship. Whitey had warned me on more than one occasion that the warlord would bring me down if he could, and having seen Northan's face as he strode angrily from the exercise cave I could only agree.

Still, I had things other than the strutting warlord to worry about.

As the weeks passed I grew almost to envy Tracy. She was with Armandra almost every day, learning the royal routine and speedily becoming the Woman of the Wind's constant companion along with Oontawa. When she was not with Armandra, Tracy spent most of her time with Jimmy. I noticed the strong bond developing between them and was pleased.

And if any member of my team was in his element, surely it was Jimmy Franklin. Apart from Tracy's attentions, he was now in a position to study the old tribes as they had really been. The Nootka and Micmac, Chimakua and Algonquin, Huron and Ojibwa, Onondaga, Chilkat, Mohawk and Tlingit; all of the northern tribes of old were represented, and Jimmy must surely have felt that he was now among the ancestors of his race.

I had asked him about the plateau's Indians, about their weapons. Why had I seen no single trace of the traditional bow and arrow? It all had to do with the nature of Borea and its people, he told me. In a world where alien, elemental powers were used as super-weapons, mere bows could easily be made useless. Temperatures could be sent down to a point where bowstrings, and even the wooden bows themselves, would break at the slightest pressure. Arrows could simply be blown aside. On the other hand, spears, harpoons and hand-axes were less susceptible to such forces.

And it was Jimmy, too, who first learned the legends of the plateau, myths that went back for something like five thousand years and maybe more. These tales had it that at a time forgotten in the dim mists of immemorial lore, Ithaqua had been prisoned in the bowels of the plateau. This had followed an act of defiance against the Elder Gods, when he had waged war on the early civilized races of Earth, striding the skies across all the dawn world and ravaging far and wide. The Wind-Walker was imprisoned thus for thousands of years before finally being released (or escaping, the legends were confused on that point) but ever since then he had been leery of the plateau, his one-time prison.

When I heard of this legend I couldn't help but tie certain facts up together. Strangely enough, Tracy featured strongly in these reckonings of mine. The fact, for instance, that my sister was the only one of all the plateau's people who possessed a positive defence against the Snow Thing; and likewise that she knew no fear when confronted with that forbidden tunnel deep in the bowels of the plateau, the tunnel whose almost physical emanations held all others back.

What lay at the other end of that dark shaft, and was it necessarily dangerous to the People of the Plateau? Tracy's star-stones, after all, were only injurious to us because we had been touched with the contamination of Ithaqua. And while we were naturally wary of the things, still they were far more dangerous – indeed lethal – to the Wind-Walker himself and his minions. Was it possible that the secret of the tunnel was that which Ithaqua also feared, the thing that held him back from destroying the plateau itself and all of its people?

Once, with Whitey, I stood at the entrance to that dark shaft, and both of us felt the thrust of forces that bade us go away or face an indefinite but very real doom. It was not only fear but a wall, a barrier real as any wall of bricks and mortar.

When I asked Whitey what he made of it, he said, 'I don't really know, Hank. I feel much the same as Tracy, I guess. On the one hand this place gives me the creeps – I don't know what's going to jump out at me, you know? – but on the other hand I feel, well, that the whole future of, oh, of *everything* is tied up at the far end of this tunnel.'

'Is that a hunch?'

'Yes, a strong one, but don't ask me to explain it. You couldn't get me down this shaft anyhow, not even for a ticket back to Earth!'

By the end of the second month I was more or less sure that Armandra had been spying on me mentally. Whether or not she was getting any clear mental pictures I did not really know; I had made no effort to project any thoughts in her telepathic direction. Nevertheless, and despite my suspicions, I stuck to my own promise not to look into her mind, though I admit that I was tempted.

Toward the end of the month, however, her prying had become so intense that I could feel her with me at almost any time in any given twenty-four hour period. At the same time I was being teased by Tracy whenever she saw me. She swore that Armandra's interest in me knew no bounds, that the Woman of the Winds had sucked her dry of all facts concerning me and my life before Borea. And I believed Tracy, for she made me promise not to repeat anything she told me; Armandra did not want me to know of her interest in me. She was no common woman to throw herself at a man.

Still, Armandra's constant presence on the borders of my mind bothered me considerably (there are things a man might want to keep secret; emotions, fears and ambitions he might not want to disclose), and so I determined to teach her a lesson if her peeking continued. It was when I had awakened from the middle of a nightmare in which I had fought to free Armandra from her father's swollen fingers, discovering her presence there at the edge of my surfacing awareness, that I found my opportunity.

'*Very well,*' I spoke to her deliberately with my mind. '*I don't know what you seek in my thoughts, Armandra, but if it is this –*' and here I projected a vivid and exceptionally erotic scene concerning the two of us, a perfectly natural fantasy which until then I had forced myself to keep out of my mind, '*– then now you know!*'

For a moment longer she was with me and I sensed sudden, explosive outrage, and something else, before she was gone. I waited a minute or two longer but

133

the ether was completely free of telepathic influences. Later I awakened again to find strange, gentle little winds caressing my body and ruffling my hair where I lay upon my bed of furs. And I knew where they came from, for beyond my stone window the grey and white Boreal scene was calm and quiet.

And so things stood for perhaps a further week, so that it was a few days into the third month when Oontawa came to bring me Armandra's invitation to the Choosing of a Champion, when a suitable mate would be found from among all the men of the plateau. I say Oontawa came with an invitation, and yet I was ready to go before she and the others of my small party brought me the news. Armandra had already uttered these words in my mind: '*Now you can come to me, Hank Silberhutte, if you want me!*'

Simply those few words, and yet every nerve in my body was suddenly energized and fires I had only guessed to exist raced in my blood, however unnaturally cold that blood might be. She had called to me, and I would go to her, yes. But on my terms.

We made our way quickly to the Hall of the Elders, and as we went Oontawa told me things I would need to know. I knew of the ritual Choosing of a Champion, but did not know the finer details of the rite. It appeared that since women were slightly in the minority, most of them were sought after as prizes by the unmarried men. Therefore a girl would usually make known to her favourite that she intended to choose a champion, and he in turn would pick a close male friend who he could trust to accept his challenge. When the girl offered herself publicly, her lover would then have to put himself forward for acceptance or rejection, and offer a challenge to anyone else who fancied the girl. His friend would then step forward and a short fight would ensue in which the 'usurper' would be 'beaten'. That was the way the ritual usually went. Usually.

This time it would be different. For one thing it was Armandra choosing a champion. For another she had made no approaches – no physical approaches, at least – to any of the plateau's males. That would have been unbecoming for first lady of the plateau. Finally, Northan had long made known his ambition to take Armandra to wife. If any man challenged his right to the Woman of the Winds, the warlord would be merciless.

We entered the Hall of the Elders to find its amphitheatre tiers of seats already filled to capacity. Young men of all the tribes jostled each other nervously just within the door, elbow to elbow with Eskimo warriors, pure whites, and mixtures of varied background and lineage. We pushed through to a clear space where I saw that a tight circle had been chalked round the base of the dais.

At the head of the dais Armandra stood, head bowed as the ritual demanded, for she must make no sign to any man in the assembly that she favoured him. She was absolutely beautiful – white as the fine furs that concealed little of the perfection of her body, the fur boots that hid the imperfection of her feet – a gorgeously carved candle of flesh crowned with the living fire of her hair.

Across the hall, in a ring of his own admirers and cohorts, stood Northan, powerfully armoured in the manner of a warlord. Yet forbidding as his armour was, the black scowl he directed all round him would surely be even more of a deterrent to anyone foolish enough to cross him in this matter.

For the moment no one in Northan's party had seen me, and from the oily smiles on the faces of his companions I could tell that they expected no interference. Well, let them expect what they would. My chill blood had been fired; Armandra meant so much to me now that death itself would be almost preferable to the thought of her in the warlord's arms.

No sooner had the thought crossed my mind than I felt Armandra's mental fingers probing. They brushed me, lingered as if to make certain of my identity, then withdrew. She trembled where she stood, then, without looking up, she spoke.

'This woman now offers herself as wife and seeks a champion. Who will fight for me, for the glory of the plateau and its people?'

Her words were hardly out before Northan stepped forward, climbed the dais steps and took Armandra's arm. Immediately the blood raced faster in my veins. Now Northan saw me; his hot eyes lingered on me for a second, then contemptuously flicked by me to sweep the hall. There was complete silence. It seemed as if the entire assembly held its breath, waiting for the warlord to speak. And he did.

'I, Northan, her champion, claim this woman, to fight for her, for the glory of the plateau and its people. Is there a man to challenge my right?' His voice itself was a threat, a promise of violent, certain death to anyone who challenged him. I felt a movement beside me in the crush of people and held back, waiting to see what this disturbance could be.

A young brave was moving forward, hawk-featured and proud, flushed with reckless excitement. Before he could reach the forward edge of the crowd a friend caught hold of him, whispering urgently, fearfully into his ear. Their eyes went to Northan where he stood watching them, an ugly grin twisting his face. Suddenly the grin dropped away and his lips hardened. His eyes bored into those of the young brave and their message was perfectly clear. So as to make it even clearer, the warlord spoke again.

'Let any challenger come forward now, and let him know that Northan fights to the death!'

Suddenly white, the young brave stepped back and quickly disappeared in the crowd, his nerve broken.

Northan's grin returned and again his fierce eyes swept the hall. And still I waited, for I knew that the ritual demanded that a challenge be made. In threatening a fight to the death, surely the warlord had put paid to any plans he might previously have made for one of his own men to take up the challenge.

Then that which I had waited for happened; Armandra's thoughts rushed in upon me. I stared at her and slowly her head lifted. She gazed straight into my eyes.

'If you hold back much longer, Hank Silberhutte, the council might declare me Northan's woman without the ritual being fully completed. They are eager to have me wed.'

'I hold back for one reason only, Armandra, and you know that reason. I would be no mate to crawl to you when you fancied me, to father your children and then be pensioned off with a seat on the Council of Elders. If I'm to be a husband then I will be a husband, not some sort of privileged lapdog!'

Now the elders of the council had moved forward to stand at the foot of the dais. They turned outward, facing the crowd. Armandra's anger flooded into my mind for an instant before she cried out; *'Oh, you fool! Do you not know why I dared not let you look into my thoughts? I am a woman, Hank Silberhutte, but a woman can have thoughts as lustful as any man!'*

And now Northan had finally seen the two of us staring intently at each other. His lips drew back in warning and his eyes slitted with fury. I felt the hate radiating from him. The spokesman of the elders stepped up beside the warlord and Armandra. He raised his arm, opened his mouth to speak –

'I challenge you, Northan,' I shouted, moving forward. 'I challenge your right to this woman and will fight you, with any weapons you choose, for the glory of the plateau and its people!'

From behind me, completely dry and without banter, I heard Whitey whisper, 'If we ever get back to Earth, that's fifty dollars you owe me, Jimmy. Never bet against a hunchman!'

Tracy breathlessly added, 'And a hundred to me. I guess you just don't know Hank, Jimmy.' Then their whispers were drowned out in the wild and amazed clamour that roared up from the thronging audience.

Part Three

1

Northan–Traitor!

(Recorded through the Medium of Juanita Alvarez)

At first I thought that Northan would explode. His mouth fell open and his eyes bulged in outrage and disbelief. He let go of Armandra's arm and began to descend the dais steps; then, noticing the way I was dressed – my sandals, soft leather trunks and fur-collared jacket – his eyes narrowed craftily. For a split second he paused, seeming to ponder something, and then his astonishment and rage appeared to increase twofold.

The spokesman of the elders had now left the dais but Northan's shout stopped him in his tracks as he hurried out of the chalked combat area. 'You there, elder! Do you see how this man mocks the Woman of the Winds, how he ridicules this ancient ceremony? He is recently come to us, and yet his attitude is not nearly what it should be. He even dares resent my authority as War-lord of the Plateau! Look at him. He is not dressed for combat, and if he were I could hardly lower myself to accept his challenge. He should not be in a position to lay claim to the lowliest, most miserable whore from the barracks areas, and yet here he is, offering himself as a mate for the Woman of the Winds! This is more than mere mockery,' his voice lifted to a bellow of artificial outrage. 'It is insolence – defilement!'

Now I knew what the warlord was up to, and as he finished speaking I saw a nodding of heads among his cronies. Even one or two of the elders seemed to be in agreement with him, much to the obvious disgust of others, particularly Charlie Tacomah. Well, Northan had

had his say, now it was my turn. Before the elder he had addressed could answer him, I spoke up.

'Elder,' I began, speaking to the same old man, 'in the Motherworld I was a leader of men, not given to accepting insults from puffed up dogs. I do not intend to lower my standards here on Borea. While it disgusts me to soil myself in combat with such as your present warlord, if that is the only way to elevate my position to one of acceptable status, I am prepared to do so.' I allowed a moment for that to sink in, then continued. 'Over and above the question of mere position, however, there is the fact that I believe I am in love with the Woman of the Winds. Because of this, I cannot stand and watch Northan take her unchallenged. If she is the prize of this contest, then I can imagine no more desirable prize. It is one which I will treasure always.' Again I briefly paused.

'I have been given to understand it is desirable that Armandra has children, that the Council of Elders has long been pressing her to wed. In the interest of the plateau I ask you this question: are your future princes to be strutting peacocks and boasters, or great men with powers as great as, and perhaps greater than their mother's own? That is the difference between Northan taking Armandra to wife, and —'

'I have heard of your so-called "powers", you dollop of —' Northan bellowed in genuine fury, until I stilled his tongue by turning my back on him. I addressed the thronging People of the Plateau now, letting them see that plainly the warlord was beneath my contempt.

'But if you, the people, or if Armandra herself has any objection to my challenging Northan, then I will withdraw my challenge, however reluctantly.'

Now this was what Northan himself had tried to do with his blustered insults; place Armandra in a position to refuse me as a prospective champion, on the grounds that I was unsuitable and beneath her contempt, without breaking any of the ceremonial rules of conduct. He had suspected something and wanted to see how the land lay between us, to see if she really did find my challenge objectionable.

She had not risen to Northan's bait; she had held her tongue. Well, I too had wanted the warlord to know the lay of the land, and so I had answered him myself, trying to force Armandra's hand. Now we both looked to her for an answer, and finally she said, 'You are both strong, able men. I have no preference, for I am the Woman of the Winds and above such things. There is no objection to either one of you, or to any man who would fight to be my champion.'

'*Liar!*' I told her with a sharp thought.

'*I cannot completely alienate the warlord,*' she answered.

'Alienate *him? He might kill me!*'

'*You must not let him – and you must not kill him! For all his strutting he leads the warriors well and is no coward in battle.*'

Meanwhile Northan had stepped slowly, menacingly down, approaching until we were face to face. I could almost see the dark thoughts revolving in his head. While he had insulted me, I had doubly insulted him; Armandra's little speech had told him nothing, had been completely unsatisfactory, merely explaining her acceptance of the ancient code. Things were not the way he would have them; his anger was now very real, and his face black as thunder. He clenched and unclenched his great hands.

'Will you not dress yourself for battle before I kill you, Earthman?' he ground the words out.

'I came into the Motherworld naked, Northan,' I told him evenly. 'These few rags should not hinder my exit from Borea, even if I were ready to make one. I choose to fight as I stand, unless your choice of weapon is the cutting whip, in which case I will dress as you are dressed.'

143

'Then let's get it over with quickly,' he snarled, hurriedly stripping himself of his armour and hurling each piece away. 'If you're afraid of the whip –'

'I don't fear the whip,' I cut him off, 'but whips are for dogs, not men.'

'Then let it be the handaxe,' he snarled. 'Either way, you die!'

Handaxes! I would rather have had unarmed combat, in which I had trained on Earth for eleven years, but if it had to be with weapons then the handaxe suited me as well as any other.

From somewhere close at hand two young Indian boys brought a golden tray bearing a pair of matched, highly decorated but nevertheless deadly, picklike handaxes. The head of each was burnished until it shone, displaying a fine cutting edge on the wide blade, and a needle tip at the end of the rearward spine. I saw that this slender, piercing spine was barbed and cut with runnels to keep blood from flowing down the shafts of the weapons to the hands of their users. I looked at the things for a long moment, and as Northan noticed the expression on my face he grinned, regaining a little of his composure.

The tray was placed on the floor between us and two more youths brought an iron chain with a manacle at each end. These clasps were secured to our left wrists. Now we were tied together, with seven or eight feet of chain between us. I waited uneasily for someone to explain the rules but apparently there were none, or I should already be in possession of them.

'Are you ready?' Armandra's voice came from the dais, trembling a little. Northan went into a crouch above the golden tray, resting the wrist of his free right hand lightly on his right knee. I followed suit. This was it then. Obviously no rules were necessary; they would be self-explanatory.

The warlord's eyes flicked sideways as he watched Armandra. I watched her too. She stood with a square of some fine weave in her hand, held high. *'When I drop the cloth, Hank Silberhutte, take up your weapon – swiftly!'*

It was an effort to stop myself nodding. I flicked my gaze from Armandra to Northan and saw the muscles standing out along his shoulders and arms; his right hand trembled over his knee in tension. Sweat suddenly burst out upon his brow. I could feel cold sweat pouring down my own face and arms.

'Now!' came Armandra's mental warning – and yet it was no real warning for she dropped the square simultaneously with her thought.

As if in slow motion I saw Northan's hand reaching down for his weapon, the glint of a razor-honed edge as the handaxe rose up and back as if with a life of its own. At the same time I took up my own weapon, feeling the shaped grip in my hand like something alive.

Then Northan jerked on the chain and I shot forward, already off balance. I saw his eyes burning fiercely as his weapon began to descend, instinctively threw myself into a dive. I passed straight between his spread legs, dragging his chained arm down and deflecting the blow he aimed at my back.

Sprawling behind him I yanked on the chain, but Northan had played this game before. He instantly tucked his head between his legs and flipped over onto his back, rolling as I directed a swift blow at the wrist of his weapon hand. My handaxe brought sparks from the floor as he jerked his wrist out of harm's way. We got to our feet together, the warlord immediately stepping forward to swing his weapon horizontally, hauling on the chain at the same time to bring me within reach.

I arched my back, felt the sharp leading edge of Northan's weapon slice a shallow groove along my belly, yanked down with my left hand to bring the warlord forward and block any backhand blow he might have planned, then leaned into a sideways swipe at his legs below the knees. He sprang high, grunting as my weapon swished through empty air.

The silence of the crowd was broken now by a succession of concerted sighings and moanings, the hissing of sharply indrawn breath. I took what little pleasure I could in the fact that what concern was being shown was mainly for me; the warlord's popularity was nothing to envy. His enemies, usually silent, were more vociferous now in the passion and excitement of the spectacle.

As we circled each other with the chain stretched between us, I noted the warlord's attitude of merciless, murderous intent. There was absolutely no doubt in Northan's mind that he would win this contest. My physical strength was greater than his, true – and he doubtless recognized that fact, however grudgingly – but his skill and experience were making me look amateurish.

So far I had been lucky: Northan had only cut me once, not seriously. Could it be that he was playing with me? Well, one way or the other, the thing must be gotten over with quickly. While the Borean warlord's skill would not diminish, my strength certainly would. In any event, brute strength can rarely compete for very long against experienced dexterity.

And as that last thought entered my head I stumbled sideways into the bottom step of the dais and went sprawling headlong. Northan had waltzed me right into it, had planned it this way, knowing I would trip myself up. All right, then let him believe that his plan had worked even better than he expected, that things were worse for me than they really were.

I forced myself to go limp on the steps. Sprawling there, I put on a look of uncomprehending, dazed bafflement. This was the work of only a second, and I never once took my eyes off the warlord.

He laughed wildly, leaping to the attack, his arms lifting to deliver the final stroke. At the last moment I threw up my own weapon to ward off the descending blow, and at the same time I threw a loop of the chain about Northan's neck. Twisting the chain, I hugged him to me.

Now I could use my strength. Gripping the chain tighter where it circled Northan's neck, I flipped him over onto his back. I locked his right arm with my own weapon and quickly trapped his right wrist in a second, smaller loop of chain. Then I applied pressure with both arms, throttling my victim while dragging him backwards up the dais steps.

Choking out curses and obscenities, the warlord flopped up the steps after me, still attempting to impale me on the spine of his weapon with repeated flicks of his trapped wrist. Near the top of the steps I put an end to that by wrapping my legs about his arm. Now his left hand stretched blindly up between my legs, reaching for me with hooked fingers. I freed my handaxe, transferred both loops of chain to my left hand and struck at Northan's left elbow with the flat of my weapon. He howled as his arm vibrated violently for a second, then flopped uselessly.

Squeezing hard and twisting the chain, I watched the warlord's face begin to go blue, purple. Slowly his right fist opened and he dropped his weapon. The handaxe went clattering down the steps. I relaxed my grip a fraction, sitting upright until I looked down into my enemy's bulging eyes. Hatred still glared out of them unconcealed.

Releasing my grip a little more, I raised my handaxe almost to arm's length and said, 'Do you admit defeat, Northan?'

For an instant indecision showed in his blood-dark features, then slyness. From his answer it was plain that he did not think I would kill him. 'It's your play, Earthman,' he gasped. 'Get it over with!'

Gritting my teeth I lifted my weapon higher yet.

The crowd gasped; Northan fainted; Armandra's voice screamed in my head: *'No!'*

I slammed the handaxe down, cutting through the knot of chain above Northan's head and sending a shower of sparks from the stone steps. Then, as a great sigh went up from the assembly, I lifted him up by his hair and put both feet to his back. Kicking him forward, I sent his unconscious body somersaulting down the steps.

'There,' I told the breathless hall as Northan landed jarringly, face down on the stone floor. 'Keep your war-lord!'

I got to my feet and stepped up beside Armandra, folding my arms and taking as dramatic a stance as I knew how. 'Keep him,' I repeated. 'Perhaps now, with his strutting stilled, he'll learn to be as good a citizen as he is a soldier.'

Then, as a delighted uproar burst out all about the hall, I said to Armandra, 'And what, princess, if Northan had killed me? It seems to me a shallow sort of affection that risks a life for a barbaric code of existence!'

She leaned on me, her beautiful face pale and drawn as death. 'Have I more faith in your friend Whitey than you?' she asked.

'Whitey? You mean you –' I sought Whitey's face in the crush of people at the foot of the dais. He was grinning cheerfully, heavy eyebrows arched happily. 'But why didn't he – why didn't *you* – tell me?'

'We did not want you to relax your vigilance for a moment.'

'Good old Whitey,' I grinned.

'He has earned my eternal respect,' she agreed. 'But if you had died, I might well have had him thrown from the roof of the plateau!'

If I had thought that now the door would be open to Armandra's chambers, then I had thought wrong. I was her champion, certainly, with the right to attend her at

148

any time during her waking hours and counsel her, and be counselled in return, but as for anything else – forget it. We could not be together; there would not be, could not be, anything other than a sort of courting between us until I had proved myself yet again, in battle against those true enemies of the plateau, the Children of the Wind. And to be absolutely sure that the opportunity would not come for us to be alone together (perhaps she did not trust herself to adhere to the plateau's ancient rules), Armandra kept either Tracy or Oontawa with her constantly.

Not only was this extremely frustrating for me but it soon began to get on Jimmy Franklin's nerves, too. Because of this, and the fact that by now Tracy was as much taken with Jimmy as he was with her, Armandra allowed the two to be together fairly regularly for short periods, but she never failed to ensure that Oontawa was there to give her moral support in Tracy's absence.

It wasn't very long before I became so unhappy with this situation that I would take myself off for long periods to the exercise cave to work off my frustrations in mock but nevertheless furious combat. Indeed, as the weeks stretched out, I began to believe – almost to fear – that all serious battling was over and done with between the People of the Plateau and the wolf-warriors of Ithaqua, that I would never again be given the chance to fight for Armandra's favours.

Certainly I did not give much thought to the possibility of any real sort of crisis developing within the plateau itself. And yet, looking back on it, I recall that there were warnings enough. Whitey was nervous and jumpy, and kept going on at me to look out for the warlord and his friends.

It was during a session in the exercise cave that Jimmy Franklin brought me word of the trouble, of Northan's treachery. Since his humiliation the warlord had slowly but surely been losing his authority with the chiefs and headmen, and now only a few of his closest friends and lieutenants remained faithful to him.

I knew of this and had already put it to Armandra that perhaps I should formally replace Northan as head of the plateau's warrior army; should become warlord in his stead. She would not hear of it. She pointed out that if Northan were deposed, stripped of rank and military power completely, this would only make him hate me more, if that were possible. Also, it would leave him free to create a variety of mischiefs on the plateau's political side. There were still those among his few cronies who, having been elevated to positions of power by the warlord, would assist him in fresh ambitions rather than risk falling into obscurity along with him. He could also compromise certain of the elders, who feared for their own positions. Even in this alien world, politics were by no means free of corruption; though from what I knew of it, Northan was at the root of everything that was bad. Well, Armandra had stressed the fact that he was ambitious . . .

I had just landed two spears in the bull from a distance of about twenty-five yards when Jimmy Franklin ran into the vast, high-ceilinged exercise cave. There was blood on the right shoulder of his fur jacket; blood dripped from a deep gash in his left thigh.

'Hank – Tracy's hurt!' he gasped it out.

'Hurt? How badly?' I grabbed him by his good shoulder, searching his face anxiously. 'What do you mean, she's hurt? Who hurt her? *How* is she hurt?'

'Northan,' Jimmy panted, 'he's defecting! He sent three of his men after Tracy. They tried to take her while she was sleeping but she woke up in time to avoid whatever they had planned. She got one of them with a star-stone. Hit him in the ear with it. Damn near burned half his head away! One of the others clubbed her unconscious. Then they split up, one heading one way to lead off any pursuit, the other making for the harbour area, where Northan's ship is tied up. He tried to take Tracy with him but it didn't work out. Her star-stones are gone, though.'

'You're not making sense,' I spoke urgently, firing questions at him. 'What do you mean, he tried to take Tracy with him? Where is she now?'

'She's all right, Hank. As luck would have it I was on my way to see her. I saw this Eskimo with her across his shoulder. That was in the perimeter tunnel leading away from our rooms. When I challenged the Eskimo he had to put her down to deal with me. We had a bit of a fight and I got a few cuts,' he indicated his shoulder and leg wounds, 'but the noise attracted a couple of Indian friends of ours. One of them was Charlie Tacomah. His room is somewhere above ours. Well, the Eskimo told Charlie that he was only carrying out Armandra's orders, but I said he must be lying. He made a run for it and Charlie brought him down with a spear. Apparently Charlie and his friend were on their way here to work out with you.'

'Right. I had arranged to meet them here. But where is Tracy now? And what about the third member of the group? And where's that dog Northan?' My voice trembled with fury.

'Charlie and his friend are taking her to Armandra. They're raising the alarm along the way. Your other questions –' he spread his arms and shrugged. 'You know as much as I do now.'

Then he swayed and half fell against me. I steadied him and noticed for the first time how much blood he was losing. I caught him as he fell and carried him to a rest couch, telling the two astonished weapon masters, 'Look after him, get him attended to immediately. I'm going to Armandra.'

On my way out I turned to Jimmy. 'Thanks for everything, Jimmy,' I said. 'Are you going to be all right?'

'I think so.'

'I reckon that Tracy's just about got to accept you as her champion now, eh?'

He managed a grin. 'She was going to anyway,' he said.

Racing through the plateau's labyrinthine ways, I could see that Charlie Tacomah had been busy alerting the entire place. Indians wearing the insignia of guardsmen were hurrying to positions at the base of the outer wall; powerfully built, squat Eskimo warriors were padding along the corridors leading to the snow-ship harbours; the entire plateau was alive to emergency measures that had been in force for hundreds of years. There was no aimless milling about; these men were moving in military precision, reacting to whatever dangers the plateau now faced, hurrying to their battle stations.

'*Hank!*' Armandra's urgent thought came to me. '*Tracy is with me now and she has just regained consciousness. Charlie Tacomah has told me what he knows. Are you coming to us? Do you know what has happened?*'

'*I'm almost with you now,*' I told her, '*and I know what happened. That dog Northan; has he really defected?*'

'*Yes, with two dozen of his officers and men. His snow-ship is no longer at its mooring. They are fleeing now across the white waste, heading for Ithaqua's altar.*'

I let my disgust at the thought of the traitor flare in my mind. '*He tried to take my sister with him, as an offering to Ithaqua, no doubt. Can we get after him? I want to be aboard the first snow-ship out of the plateau.*'

'*You cannot, Hank,*' she answered as I raced by her Eskimo guardsmen and their bears. '*We are making no pursuit. My father, Ithaqua, is back on Borea. Northan was waiting for him to return. He chose the hour of his treachery well.*'

'*Then the dog gets clean away?*'

'*Not so,*' ominous undertones showed in her thought patterns. '*I am sending a wind after him even now!*'

I ducked through the curtains and entered Armandra's chambers. Oontawa was tending to Tracy who lay propped up on a couch. My sister had a bump like a hen's egg on the side of her head. Armandra, eyes closed and face grim, head tilted back, held out her arms before her while her hands described forward, stirring motions.

'Armandra,' I began, stepping forward. But at that precise moment her entire face started to glow bloodred while the hair of her head rose up to undulate above her as in an updraught of air. A wind blew out from her, thrusting me aside as it raced across the room to set the curtains flapping violently. A moment more this phenomenon continued, then Armandra's hair settled down again, the flush left her face, the wind ceased. She lowered her hands and opened her eyes.

'Come,' she said. 'We will see what games my familiars can play with Northan's snow-ship.'

'Wait,' I answered, hurrying through into a second room, Armandra's resting chamber, to fetch my binoculars. Then we went out, back along the corridor to the viewing balcony with its widely spaced bars. Tracy and Oontawa followed us. I put an arm around my sister and asked her if she was all right.

'Yes. A bit dizzy, that's all. That was quite a bump I took.'

'Not nearly as painful as the bump I'll deal the ex-warlord when next we meet!' I promised her.

'*If* you meet him again Hank,' Armandra grimly put in. We had arrived at the balcony and now she pointed out through the bars. 'See . . .'

Through the binoculars I saw the snow-ship fleeing, already two-thirds of the way to the circle of totems with its central altar. Atop that altar I could see the Snow Thing, and he too was watching the snow-ship's progress. At that distance the monster's outline was indistinct, but the flaring of his eyes was clearly discernible. I turned my binoculars back to the snow-ship, seeing that the vessel fairly leaped across the snow.

'See,' Armandra said again, 'the winds are answering my father's call and Northan's ship flies on their wings. But I, too, have sent a wind, one to vex the warlord's flight!'

Now, building up behind the snow-ship, growing out of the frozen white surface of the plain, the grey funnel of a tornado raised itself up, twisting and bending furiously as it rushed down upon the fleeing vessel. Closer to the ship the pursuing tornado roared, the howling of its passage coming back to us like the mad wail of some vengeful god.

Then Armandra cried out in anger and frustration, 'Ah! My father is curious . . . he joins the play . . . Ithaqua displays his power!'

And sure enough the figure atop the pyramid altar had held up a massive hand to the onrushing tornado, and with a sweeping contemptuous gesture he *brushed it aside!*

The tornado, towering high and threateningly over the snow-ship, suddenly swerved aside and teetered crazily, blindly in the wrong direction. The snow-ship sped on. Armandra began to close her eyes, set her jaw stubbornly and raised her arms – then shook her head and let her arms fall.

'What is the use?' she asked. 'He is not to be denied his mastery of the winds.'

Out over the white waste the tornado came to an abrupt halt. Ithaqua, from atop his pyramid altar, dismissed it with a wave of his hand. It collapsed in upon itself and spilled to the ground as a fine haze of snow and ice particles.

'But won't Ithaqua kill Northan and his crew?' I asked.

'No, Hank,' Armandra turned to me. 'Northan was the plateau's warlord; he knows all of the secret ways, the many tunnels that lead from the base of the plateau to its halls, barracks, recreation caves and dwellings. He will be a mine of information to Ithaqua's priests and soldiers. When they are ready, he will lead them against the plateau, have no doubt of it.'

'Will he try to come back for you?'

She shook her head grimly. 'No, my father would never allow it. He would destroy everyone on Borea first. Ithaqua is a lonely creature, Hank. He desires a friend to walk the winds between the worlds with him.' For a moment her face glowed with a strange passion. 'And sometimes,' her voice was suddenly far away, 'sometimes –'

Without knowing why I felt a strange chill grip me. Instinctively I focused upon the horror atop the distant altar. His eyes were burning brightly, staring directly at the plateau. I knew then that he saw us, if not physically, certainly with his mind.

'Stop that!' I cried, taking the Woman of the Winds into my arms and kissing her tenderly. 'Stop it. You're not his, Armandra, you're mine!'

She clung to me gratefully, drank of my strength, and an anger blew up in me that led almost to disaster. Without thinking I put her behind me, gripped the wide bars of the balcony with both hands and stared straight out at Ithaqua.

I screamed at him with my mind. *'You great, loathsome, alien blasphemy! When the day of reckoning comes, may the Elder Gods burn out your black heart and float your soul on a sea of fire, to fry until the end of time! Until then, know this. Your daughter is mine, mine! and neither man nor monster can ever take her from me!'*

The defiant gesture of a spoiled child! But not satisfied with that, I also conjured up a mental picture of a star-stone of ancient Mnar and, hurling that at him too, added intended injury to the insult.

Immediately, violently, the thing at the apex of the ice altar reacted. First I sensed his mental derision at the star-stone symbol, as if he already knew that we were no longer in possession of the stones; then came his anger as he lifted his arms up to the grey skies and expanded, bulging upward and outward until he towered fully a hundred feet into the air; and finally he stepped aloft to walk up the wind, reaching into the suddenly boiling sky to draw down weirdly flickering lightnings that played in his hands. For a moment longer he held that inferno of electrical energies in his hands.

'*Back!*' came Armandra's warning cry. 'Back from the bars!' She tugged at my arm until I followed her at a run, pushing Tracy and Oontawa in front of me. We had covered only a few paces when a weird, hissing blue light filled the balcony and corridor. Then the hissing became a deafening crackling as a large hand picked me up and hurled me headlong. The two girls flew with me – but not Armandra.

From where I dazedly lay I looked back at the Woman of the Winds, and at the balcony beyond her. Her hands were held up against the blue light which flickered angrily about her but did her no harm. Lightning played about the bars of the balcony, heating them a glowing white and running in rivers of sparks all about the floor, ceiling and walls. Tongues of flickering fire reached hungrily after us, but were held back by Armandra's power. For a moment longer the scene seared itself upon my mind, then the blaze of electrical fire died away.

In my mind's eyes I pictured a horrific figure striding in icy air over Borea, throwing back his head to roar with glee; then that vision too was gone and I was left knowing that Ithaqua had sent it.

Armandra came to me as I got to my feet. Chidingly she said, 'That was no way to talk to the Wind-Walker.' Then she hugged and kissed me, glad that no harm had come to me. Obviously she had heard what I said to her monstrous father, and it seemed she was no longer so vehemently opposed to someone's laying claim to her, provided I was that someone.

She kissed me again and with her kisses came a great yearning inside me. She sensed it and held me away at arm's length, turning her head confusedly to where the women had now regained their feet. She disengaged herself, asking them if they were hurt in any way. They were not.

Then, watching me out of the corner of her eye, in a very low tone she said, 'You must be very careful, Hank, how you taunt or tempt a being with the power to hurl the very lightning of the storm against you. Be it Ithaqua or Ithaqua's daughter!'

The yearning in me doubled as I saw again the mischief floating to the surface of her ocean eyes. She quickly sobered. 'Come,' she said. 'We will return to my rooms and wait for news.'

2

How Many Tomorrows?

(Recorded through the Medium of Juanita Alvarez)

News was not long in coming. An Eskimo guard soon arrived and, with much bowing and scraping, was let into Armandra's chambers. 'Good, good,' she said, drawing him upright and cutting short the formalities. 'What news?'

She listened intently to his rather slow, guttural speech – words meaningless to me, for where she had spoken in English he answered in *Eskimo* – until he was done, then dismissed him. In all of his short report I had caught only one phrase, a phrase repeated in something akin to awe and horror: 'The Madness!'

As the guardsman bowed himself out Armandra turned to me. 'They have caught the third traitor, the one who took Tracy's star-stones. He was hiding in the forbidden tunnel.'

'In the tunnel?' I repeated. 'Hiding there?' I frowned, shaking my head. 'But how could any man of the plateau ever manage to steal Tracy's star-stones in the first place? And I thought no man could ever venture into the forbidden tunnel, that its emanations were impenetrable. Now you tell me this man was hiding there!'

'Perhaps not *hiding*, then,' she looked at me pointedly. 'No, he was – trapped – there. I do not care to think about it. They had him cornered and he had only one way to go. They caught him when he came out. As for the star-stones, that was simple. He caught them up at the end of his spear, lifted them by their chains, kept them away from him so they could not harm him.'

'Even so,' I said, 'he must be a very brave man. Brave and misguided.'

'A frightened man,' she answered. 'Frightened of Northan.'

'I want to see him, question him,' I told her. 'I want to discover Northan's intentions, what he's up to.'

She shook her head. 'You'll get no sense out of him, Hank. The history of the plateau tells that once, hundreds of years ago, offenders against the common good, thieves and the like, were driven into the forbidden tunnel as punishment for their crimes. The records all show the same end result. It will be the same now; this underling of Northan's, he will not be – coherent.'

The way she said the last word found me looking at her inquiringly, but she avoided my eyes. She did not like to talk about that enigmatic tunnel in the bowels of the plateau, or of its effect upon men.

Tracy spoke up. 'And have they got the star-stones back?'

Armandra shook her head. 'No, he must have left them behind him, in that place. If so, they will remain there forever.'

At that point there came again the sound of padding feet from the corridor. Oontawa went out and returned after a few seconds. 'The man is being held in the council hall,' she told her mistress. 'The elders have tried to question him, in vain. Now they ask what you want done with him.'

Armandra began to answer, then checked herself. She turned to me. For a long moment she looked at me. Finally she said to Oontawa: 'That is not a matter for me. Better you speak to the warlord.'

For a moment Oontawa looked puzzled, but then understanding dawned in her eyes. Of course. Now there was a new warlord! Speaking to me, the girl repeated, 'The elders are holding the man; has the warlord any instructions?'

'I'll come to see him,' I told her, 'and I'll talk to the elders, too. Send word that I'll be there shortly.'

Oontawa left immediately and Tracy went with her. My sister knew that Jimmy Franklin had been hurt and wanted to go to him. Finally I was alone with Armandra. Now she relaxed a little, became a woman again and not a goddess.

'Big trouble is coming, Armandra,' I said. 'We don't need a hunchman to tell us that much.'

'I know,' she answered. 'And I think – I think that I am frightened, Hank. Things are all coming to a head too soon, too quickly. Troubles pile up all about us. The plateau's problems seem about to engulf us all. And now you have accepted a task that might daunt any man. You are the plateau's new warlord, and at a time such as this!'

'This was the way it had to happen,' I answered. 'In a way I'm glad. It's my chance to prove myself once and for all – to the People of the Plateau and to you. You know what that means to me.' I forced myself to grin, making light of things, kissing her forehead while she clung to me.

Her voice was molten gold when she said, 'We may not have much time, Hank. That is what frightens me most.'

'We've wasted a lot of time,' I answered, fires melting my iced blood. She pushed me away, her face suddenly flushed.

'When you have spoken to the elders, return to me,' she hurriedly said. 'Make what arrangements you must – do what must be done – then come back.' She opened her mind to me: *visions of lurking, half-formed fears and fierce, tumultuous passions!*

'I am your warrior, Armandra, your champion, but not yet truly your husband. What of the plateau's rules? The ancient codes?'

The flush left her face and disbelief replaced it. Thunderheads darkened her brows and lightning flashed in her eyes. '*Dare* you make excuses when I have offered –?'

'But the ancient codes!' I protested, unable now to contain my laughter.

'Codes! Rules!' she started to flare up, then burst out laughing with me when she realized I was playing. Suddenly we both sobered, and I saw that her eyes were now wantonly seductive, Icelandic pools beneath which volcanic fires roared. 'We will have to forget the rules, Hank.'

'Armandra –'

'*No!*' she broke away from me. 'Go to the elders now, then come back to me.'

On my way to the Hall of the Elders I found myself shadowed by two lean, powerful Indians who took up a steady, loping walk at my heels. I began to feel alarmed when it dawned on me that these could be two more of Northan's men, left behind to take care of me.

After they had followed me for at least half the distance to my destination, when it seemed that they were stealthily closing the gap between us, I turned on them. I drove my elbow deep into the stomach of the one on my right, snatching his handaxe from his belt as he doubled over, retching. Dropping to a crouch and twisting into a good position to deliver a low, killing kick at the second of the two, I was stopped dead in my tracks by the sight of the man prostrate upon the tunnel floor!

I took away his handaxe and hauled him to his feet, demanding to know what was going on. He had a fair grasp of English, speaking to me rapidly, babbling while his companion slowly managed to compose himself. They were my personal bodyguards and messengers, sent by Oontawa to attend me.

I offered my apologies and clumsily attempted to brush the winded Indian down. He assured me that he considered himself the recipient of a great honour; he could now claim to have seen and experienced the lightning ferocity of 'Sil-ber-hut-te' at first hand. His children's children

161

would talk about me, and he, Kasna'chi, would be a part of my legend. He would doubtless have gone on had I not stopped him. It is disconcerting to say the least to find oneself growing into a living legend!

And so, with Kasna'chi and Gosan-ha close at my heels, I eventually arrived at the Hall of the Elders. The Indians waited outside while I went in to see the elders and their prisoner.

Other than the ten elders, two Eskimo guardsmen were also present in the great cave. The latter pair held between them a man who had plainly been of French–Canadian extraction. They were not so much detaining him as holding him up. I mention him in the past tense because quite simply he was no longer – anything; whatever he had been, he was no longer.

Though his body showed few of the normal signs of age, his face was deeply lined, his hair visibly greying. His eyes bulged and stared blankly and a slack grin or grimace made his lower lip seem to droop. Saliva ran down his chin. He babbled quietly, incoherently to himself. Armandra was quite right. No one would ever again get any sense out of this man.

I had him taken away. His guards were to give him into the hands of those who would do what could be done for him. Useless to punish a man who could not remember his crime, could remember nothing at all.

Then I spoke to the elders, placing emphasis on the plateau's near invulnerability, making light of Northan's defection and stating that we were all now better off without him. I told them I doubted the ex-warlord's immediate ability to attack us, that for the moment we had nothing to fear from him. While I was delivering my pep-talk, Charlie Tacomah caught my eye. When I had done he drew me to one side.

'I see what you are doing,' he told me, 'and it is good, but I hope you are not fooling yourself. Northan knows

162

all of the plateau's intricacies, its strong defensive positions and its weak spots. Until now we have been fortunate; the great majority of the Wind-Walker's people have been weak-willed and ignorant. Northan is neither of these things. At last Ithaqua has an ally he can use.'

'And I have allies, too, Charlie,' I answered. 'You are one of them. The elders will have to do without you from now on. Tactician you once were, tactician you will be again. You are more use to me right now than to the elders.'

'What do you want me to do?'

'I want you to start by having a good look at the plateau's defences. Find me all the weak spots and devise ways to protect them. And I want to know our vantage points and cave entrances which can be made impregnable, but from which special forces might make telling forays. I need to know these things in order to prepare a plan of defence. In fact I want you to prepare such a plan, and the sooner you get started the better.'

His eyes had taken on a keen glint as I talked; a new fire now shone out of them. 'Do you think that the attack will come soon?'

'As soon as Northan can turn Ithaqua's rabble into an army, yes. They have their rough edges, the wolf-warriors, but those can soon be hammered out. I've seen them in battle and I was impressed. Led by Northan, backed up by the Wind-Walker's hellish powers – oh, yes, it's certainly coming, Charlie. I want us to be ready, that's all. If only there was a way we could get those star-stones back.'

He shook his head at that. 'If they have been left in the forbidden tunnel as we fear, then they cannot be recovered. They must – simply – remain –' He checked himself in mid-sentence, brightening. 'But wait! Haven't I heard your sister say that –'

'Forget it!' I snapped. 'She may not be afraid of the tunnel but I certainly am, for myself and for Tracy. If there's something down there that can do what we've seen done to a man – something that turns my bones to jelly just standing at the entrance to its lair – then I'm not asking my sister to face it!'

'Of course not,' he quickly replied. 'It was a stupid thing to suggest.' After a pause he added, 'I have a lot to do now, and you will be even more occupied. If you will excuse me –'

'Yes, Charlie. And let me have the answers as soon as you know them.'

After Charlie left the Hall of the Elders I had a few more words with the council before setting out to look for Whitey. It dawned on me that I had not laid eyes on him for four or five days. I wondered what he was up to, and I wanted his advice. He was my hunchman, and if anyone ever needed a few decent hunches it was me.

I found myself wondering: what kind of a hunchman was Whitey anyway? Oh, he'd warned me often enough about Northan, certainly, but there had been nothing specific, nothing definite. Whitey must be losing his touch. Soon enough I was to find out just how right I was.

Then, realizing that I need not look for Whitey myself, I sent Kasna'chi to find him, keeping Gosan-ha with me when I went to the roof of the plateau for a breath of fresh air.

All around the great flat roof, massive battlements had been cut from the solid rock. Behind them, spaced at intervals of about one hundred yards, keen-eyed watchers observed the white waste from this supreme vantage point. The scene to the front of the plateau was one which, despite its monochrome sterility, perhaps because of it, seemed starkly beautiful to me. Only one thing marred it: the obscene fingers of the distant totems pointing at a leaden sky, circling the pyramid altar like dancers frozen in some evil ritual.

And the being atop the pyramid seemed frozen too, as he motionlessly surveyed the strangely littered terrain of his territory, the white waste. A rage quickly built up in me and I had to force myself to carefully put down the binoculars, clipping them to my belt. It wouldn't do to drive the Wind-Walker into another frenzy, not while I was up here.

My mind was a muddle of conflicting thoughts, all of then having to do with the plateau's safety and future. Finally I left the roof. I walked with my thoughts, measuring the rock corridors until, almost without realizing it, I found myself on the penultimate level. There, at that entrance where Eskimo guardsmen stood in rich ceremonial robes with their bears shuffling behind them, I awoke to my surroundings. Deep in thought though I had been, busy with mad flights of heroic fancy as well as very real plans for the protection of the plateau, my feet had led me back to Armandra.

I dismissed Gosan-ha there, leaving orders with the guardsmen that I was not to be disturbed unless it was a matter of the gravest urgency, and then I went on along the richly furnished corridor.

The next morning, Oontawa awakened us. She was shocked and it showed on her face. Armandra took charge of the situation at once, saying, 'Oontawa, do you disapprove? This is my husband that fought for me in the Choosing of a Champion. Yes, and I love him.'

'Yes, Armandra,' the Indian girl began, 'but –'

'There may be very little time left for us,' Armandra interrupted. 'In the battle that must soon come we may be the losers. It is not a thought I want spread among my people but the possibility exists. You are just a maiden, a girl who has been friend and companion to me and who loves me. I love you too, for your innocence. Though not too many years separate us, our minds are centuries apart.

I am old in strange wisdom and you are innocent. In your innocence I have seen you smile favourably upon a certain brave. Is it not so?'

'It is so,' Oontawa bowed her head and flushed.

'And is he not the handsome brave that keeps the bears for our warlord? His name is –'

'Kota'na, my princess.'

'Just so. Then I repeat that time is very precious, Oontawa. I suggest we arrange a Choosing of Champions for you. As of this moment you are dismissed from my service, but I know you will remain my friend. Go, girl, and find your happiness, as I have found mine.'

Oontawa bowed again and when she lifted her head there were glad tears in her eyes. She turned to me. 'Lord Sil-ber-hut-te, your friend Whitey waits to see you. He is with Gosan-ha and Kasna'chi. They wait where the guardsmen stand with their bears.'

I smiled and nodded. 'I will come.'

Oontawa waited on the far side of the curtained doorway that closed off Armandra's rooms, and when I was ready we walked together to the guarded end of the corridor where Whitey and my bodyguards waited. She left me there to go in search of Kota'na, taking him the news that Armandra had ended her service so that the Keeper of the Bears could take her to wife.

I walked with Whitey, slowly pacing the fantastic labyrinths of the plateau and talking to him while my bodyguards kept a discreet distance to the rear. Whitey was up-to-date on everything, had heard of my new office, was pleased that Armandra had placed the might of the plateau in my hands. He said as much, and yet I sensed that something was bothering him.

'I feel I've kind of let you down this time, Hank,' he finally said after a long period of silence. 'Something – I don't know what – isn't right.'

'How do you mean, Whitey?'

'It's hard to explain, a funny thing. And yet not so funny, if you follow me. All my life, even before I was fully aware of this power of mine to, well, to gauge the mood of the future, so to speak, before I was a hunchman proper, I could kind of *sense the existence* of tomorrow. I was as much aware of the reality of the future as other people were of the past. Tomorrow was as certain to me as yesterday.' He paused for a moment, then continued, 'I suppose it must be a difficult concept for anyone who's not a hunchman. Anyway, as I've grown older the impressions of tomorrow have occasionally been clearer. Such flashes have been my hunches of course, the end results of the special talent that made me valuable to the Wilmarth Foundation. Until recently . . .'

'Oh.' I frowned. 'Well, go on, Whitey. What's the problem?'

He shrugged resignedly. 'It's a worrying thing, Hank. I feel like I just lost a leg or something. You know what I mean?'

'No more hunches, eh?'

'Right the first time. Sorry, Hank.'

'But how could it happen? Have you any ideas?'

'Yeah, I have an idea,' he grimly answered. 'My idea is, how can I see tomorrows that aren't going to be?'

'Not going to be? There'll always be tomorrows, Whitey.'

'Sure,' he said. 'But will we be here to enjoy them?'

3

The Lull Before the Storm

(Recorded through the Medium of Juanita Alvarez)

The next fortnight was one of frantic activity. Working to
Charlie Tacomah's suggestions I garrisoned soldiers close
to the plateau's outer walls, in temporary cavern-barracks
from which they could rapidly deploy to defensive positions. The plateau's weak spots – several large and easily
accessible entrances opening straight into the guts of the
plateau from the plain – were specially strengthened and
fortified to my orders. Quarriers worked nonstop to cut
and lever massive blocks of stone into place. We did a
similar job with the snow-ship keeps, those fjordlike,
frozen reentries where the great skiborne battlecraft were
harboured. These tasks, wherever possible, I personally
supervised. If I was not available, Charlie was there in my
stead. With each and every person in the plateau realizing
the urgency of the situation, the work went ahead with
very few complications; the plateau's peoples were all
right there behind their princess – yes, and behind their
new warlord, too.

Heartening as all this was, over that same period of time
there were worrying things happening out on the white
waste in the vicinity of the Wind-Walker's temple. The
watchers on the roof of the plateau had reported the activity; I myself had seen it enlarged in my binoculars. The
Children of the Winds had gathered from far and wide,
were exercising in orderly military manoeuvres across
the frozen terrain of their territory. Northan was flexing
his new and savagely powerful muscles, making a vast
and disciplined fighting body out of the entire nation

of Ithaqua's worshippers. And always the Snow-Thing watched over the ex-warlord's progress, and always the tension heightened.

Then, during the third week, there were two new developments. Ithaqua departed yet again, walking away across the winds and disappearing over Borea's rim, and Jimmy Franklin brought me news of that which I could only consider an act of sheerest lunacy. The latter concerned Tracy.

It was midweek and I was with Armandra, who was trying to explain to me her alien father's eternal wanderlust, his apparent inability to remain in any specific sphere for any appreciable length of time, which she explained as being simply one of the conditions of the limited freedom allowed him by the Elder Gods, when Jimmy came to us. He breathlessly told us his story.

He and my sister had been walking together through the complexes of the plateau when their wanderings had taken them to the forbidden tunnel. They had stood together at that dark entrance, and suddenly he had noticed a new light in Tracy's eyes. She was aware, of course, that her star-stones were believed to be somewhere in that sinister burrow, left there by Northan's now incurably crazed underling.

Realizing what she intended to do, Franklin had tried to stop her but discovered he was neither physically nor mentally strong enough to do so. His wounds had healed, true, but his strength was not yet back to normal. When she broke loose from him and ran off down the tunnel, bearing with her a torch snatched from the nearest flambeau, he had tried to follow her but was held back by the dreadful *power* emanating from that hideous shaft. It had been as if he threw himself against the solid wall of some castle of evil, while a brain-eating acid was dripped upon his head from the unseen battlements.

Finally, reeling and clutching at his sanity where the *power* had brought him to a halt just a few paces inside the nightmare entrance – knowing that to remain would certainly mean succumbing to madness – he realized that he could do nothing at all to help Tracy. She would not return until she either found the star-stones or satisfied herself that they were not there. Then Franklin crawled from the place on all fours, and as soon as he had recovered he hurried to me.

We returned to the forbidden tunnel immediately, Armandra and my bodyguards with us, and on our way I obtained a slender spear. Seeing that I had armed myself, Armandra clung desperately to my arm and I felt her mental fingers worriedly probing the edges of my telepathic consciousness. I closed my mind to her, though already she must have known what I intended to do – what I would at least attempt.

I expected objections but at the tunnel mouth no one tried to stop me; it would have been futile to do so. I simply ran into the tunnel, a burning brand in one hand, my spear in the other, shouting Tracy's name. And immediately the *power* was there pushing against me, trying to hold me back with fingers of fear that worked in my brain, so that with every step I felt I was leaping from a precipice, or hurling myself down the living throat of some primordial reptile. And the echoes of my cries came back to me: 'Tracy! . . . Tracy! . . . *Tracy!*'

And then I was on my knees, pushing forward, spear and torch before me, with shadows leaping on the walls and ceiling like mad demons while fear tore at my insides. And I knew I was going to go mad with fear. I knew it.

And I would have gone mad if I had forced myself on – but I didn't have to. From around a bend in the tunnel It came, waves of fear beating out from It, the horror that the plateau dreaded, hitherto unseen, unknown.

Manlike It was, an inky anthropomorphic blot that dripped namelessly; but small as I could never have expected it to be, this Thing that radiated such *fear*!

As It came closer I backed away on all fours, dropping my torch from nerveless fingers, feeling the fear eating my brain. And then I remembered Tracy.

'Monster!' I screamed. I got to my feet, drew back my arm and balanced the slender spear, which the instinct for self-preservation had made me hold on to, aiming at the thing's heart –

And the monster spoke!

'Hank? Is that you? Are you all right?'

Tracy! But if this was my sister, why should I feel the *fear* radiating from her? Why should my stomach twist and writhe with every step she took toward me?

I backed away, noting through waves of terror how the inky figure kept well away from the sputtering flame as it edged around the still burning torch where it flared upon the floor. With every step the figure advanced I had to retreat, pushed back by the *fear*.

'Tracy.' I somehow managed to force words from my parched throat. 'Is it really you? What's happened to you?'

'Of course it's me, Hank,' the figure replied, and certainly it spoke with Tracy's voice. 'Yes, it's me. I'm covered in oil, that's all.'

'But Tracy,' I pressed her, still backing away, 'why – why am I *afraid* of you?'

'What?' she stopped moving toward me and I detected the growing concern and disbelief in her voice. A moment later she laughed and I knew at last that it really was Tracy. 'Oh, it must be the star-stones!' she said in sudden relief. 'I came down here to look for two of them – and I found hundreds! Down at the other end of the tunnel there's a huge cavern, with star-shaped symbols on the walls and all over the ceiling, and the floor is literally covered with the stones. I'm carrying dozens of them with me right now, and they're heavy! It must be the stones you can sense; you're frightened of *them*, not me.'

She was right, of course she was. 'And this cavern,' I questioned, still retreating before her. 'Is it – empty?'

'Yes, apart from the star-stones and the oil. At one place the cavern wall is cracked and oil is seeping in, I guess from the place where the plateau's people draw off their fuel. I left my torch stuck in the floor while I was gathering up some of the stones. Then I slipped and fell in the oil. That's why I had to leave the torch behind and come back in the dark. Are you all right, Hank?'

Now it was my turn to laugh, weakly, almost hysterically. 'Oh, yes, I'm all right – but you'd better let me warn the others or they're likely to make a pincushion of you as you come out.'

'Yes, yes do!' she cried. 'Oh, go on, Hank, get out of here. You sound dreadful. Please hurry on ahead. And don't worry. There's absolutely nothing down here to hurt you. Oh, except the star-stones, of course.'

Of course. Nothing but the star-stones!

I turned then and ran, or rather I staggered, back along the way I had come. And all the way the *fear* snapped at my heels, right behind me. Only now I knew exactly what I was afraid of – what everyone in the plateau had feared – and though the knowledge made no difference and I was still desperately afraid, I was also jubilant!

'Let them come,' my spirit cried inside me, 'and Ithaqua with them. At least the odds are balanced a lot more in our favour now!'

And that brings us up to five days ago, Juanita. I've probably missed things, I know, but nothing that I think is of any real importance. Let's see now, how long have we been in touch? With time off for a few breaks and a couple of hours sleep, I reckon it must have been all of thirty-six hours. Is that a record for telepathic contact between worlds – or – rather, between 'spheres'? I suppose it must be. You say Peaslee has given you a team of stenographers, typists, tape recorders? Methodical as ever. He doesn't miss a trick.

With you right now? Yes, I see in your mind that he is. He says to quit the casual chatter and get on with it, does he? Well, you can tell him from me that the Wilmarth Foundation doesn't carry much weight way out here on Borea. He's right, though, so I suppose we'd better get on with it. Not that there's a lot left to tell.

We're simply waiting now, there's nothing else to do. Armandra has been resting for two days, seeing no one, not even me. She says she'll need all her strength for the coming fight, and try as I might I can't convince her that she won't have any part of it. The trouble is, I know that if she wanted to join in there's not much I could do to stop her; she would only be fighting for her people after all. And for her freedom.

It can't be far off now, the fight, for Northan has quit exercising his army and holds it in readiness. And Ithaqua is back. The Wind-Walker perches atop his pyramid as always, except that he no longer stares out and away over the white wastes. Now he faces squarely in the direction of the plateau.

Tracy has been busier than anyone else since she found the star-stones in the cave at the end of the forbidden tunnel, those same star-stones that once held the Wind-Walker imprisoned deep in the guts of the plateau. That's why the horror has always held the plateau in great respect, why he himself has not yet seen fit directly to attack the place.

But to get back to Tracy: she must have walked miles, poor kid, before she let Kota'na talk her into riding one of his bears. Since then she's been getting about much faster. And her work is probably the most important of all, for Tracy has been putting the finishing touches to the plateau's defences.

I suppose I could say that the idea was a group effort of Charlie Tacomah, Tracy and myself – but the truth is that Tracy's had the lion's share of the work. I had a rough idea how I wanted the star-stones used; Charlie worked out the mechanical details; Tracy is still working to finish it off, but it's just about done now.

Roughly the idea was this: that the stones be used as a secondary defence behind the new tunnel barriers, to deny entry into the plateau should the barriers be breached. Charlie designed heavy wooden frames, had them built and suspended from the ceilings of the outer tunnels. Fixed to the fronts of these frames are spears set in two rows. The bottom row consists of conventional spears fixed about two feet apart, and these are meant to impale the giant wolves. The upper rows are less conventional; in fact they're not spears at all but simply stout poles, like slender battering rams. Only nailed to the end of each pole is a star-stone – and these are not meant for wolves . . .

Tracy's hands are a mass of blisters. Because she's the only one able to handle the star-stones, by now she must have nailed up almost two hundred of the things.

Anyway, Charlie's devices work like this: swinging from the ceilings of the tunnels and operated by teams of men hauling on ropes from the rear, they should form impassable barriers. The spears are not barbed; that is, they will impale men and wolves alike, but their victims will not pile up on the shafts. By the time a wall of bodies has built up in front of one of these fearsome devices, well, the passage will be impassable by then anyway. And when they are not in use the spear-frames can be hauled up to the tunnel ceilings to allow my warriors passage beneath them.

There have been one or two minor accidents when Tracy's assistants have come into momentary contact with her stones, but once burned means twice shy. Those who suffer make sure they don't get burned a second time! I imagine that when these terrible weapons are in action, nothing Ithaqua can send against them will stand a chance.

And that is only one of the uses to which the star-stones have been put. They've also been fixed on the massive gates that guard the snow-ship keeps, and they form a five-pointed design in the battlements of the plateau's roof. All in all, I believe we've used them to their best advantage. Time alone will tell, and I think there's precious little time left.

Speaking for myself, I would prefer to hold back when the battle starts, let the Children of the Winds come to me and make them fight on my terms, but my generals tell me that to do so would be to severely demoralize the warriors of the plateau. To many of the young braves this seems their golden opportunity to distinguish themselves in bloody battle. I daren't deny them that which is their right according to the plateau's ancient codes and customs. That's why, before Ithaqua returned, I had the snow-ships out exercising and manoeuvring all about the foot of the plateau, while Armandra sent fair winds to fill their sails.

Thus, when the time comes, they will go out to attack the wolf-warriors and their battle-sledges. At the same time, foot soldiers and mounted bears will protect the tunnel entrances and keeps, while the fortified positions will be manned by strong but older men who are past their prime. Then, if things go badly, survivors of the fighting will fall back with the wounded and take over the plateau's defensive positions. They will be replaced in the field of battle by reserves, while the wounded will be passed back along the tunnels to first-aid and hospital centres. The crews of the snow-ships will simply have to fend for themselves if their vessels are wrecked, getting back to the safety of the plateau as best they can.

But I need not go on. All of this is prearranged. The plan in its entirety is complicated and would be meaningless to you, Juanita, unless you knew the plateau as I now know it; which is why I have only given you the basic outline. Now we wait.

Jimmy has just been to see me, excited about a device he's had built and positioned in the mouth of a small cave fifty feet above ground level. It's a powerful catapult on a swivelling base. He and Tracy have been practising with pebbles and they can now accurately land a stone – a *star*-stone when the time comes – almost anywhere inside a two hundred-and-fifty-yard radius. Jimmy will aim and release the 'shells', Tracy will load for him. Now she's gone off yet again to the forbidden tunnel to replenish her stock of stones.

Meanwhile, I've managed to convince Armandra that she must stay out of the fight. She promises not to join the battle unless Ithaqua himself takes a strong hand. I can't really picture him trying to do that once he sees what we have waiting for his wolf-warriors. Of course, there was a condition to Armandra's agreement to stay out of things: I have to keep out of it too, despite the fact that I've a personal score to settle with Northan. It was the only way I could make Armandra see sense.

So here I am right now where I've positioned myself in an observation cave a third of the way up the face of the plateau, surrounded by a gang of runners who will take my commands below to the fighting men once the battle begins. It's a pretty basic system of communication, but the best I can do.

And that's our present position. Jimmy and his catapult, along with a couple of runners and assistants of his own, are below me on the face of the plateau and about one hundred yards to my right, where Tracy should soon be joining them. Whitey should be up on the roof, still desperately trying to get a peek into the future and keeping a keen eye on the now very much increased activity out across the white waste. Armandra is high above in her rooms, no doubt still nervously fretting. The warriors and their bears are resting up in temporary quarters and barracks down below, and the crews of the snow-ships are ready to man their vessels at a moment's notice, though I can't see them doing a great deal if Ithaqua decides to blow in the wrong direction. That's the trouble with this situation; nothing is certain, everything is a bif *if* – everything except the one really definite fact that Ithaqua *will* send the Children of the Winds against us.

Now I'm going to stop sending, Juanita. There are a few last details I have to see to. I'll contact you again when I can, or when there's something to report.

NOTE: Following this last telepathic transmission from Hank Silberhutte, which ended at 10 A.M., June 5, nothing further was heard from him until 2 P.M. the next day. Then, from across unknown gulfs of space and time, Juanita Alvarez again began to receive his thoughts. The following, final recordings, forming as they do the last part of this document, were commenced at that time.

Part Four

1

The Assault Begins

(Recorded through the Medium of Juanita Alvarez)

Whitey is dead, crushed and destroyed as if he had never been, *removed* as he gave all he had, his very life, to save Armandra from her dreadful father and the alien star-voids he eternally wanders. Armandra is hurt, perhaps crippled, I don't know yet. The physicians are with her now.

Tracy and Jimmy are safe, and I'm thankful for that, but Paul White . . . poor Whitey. No wonder he could see no more tomorrows, no futures; for him there was no future.

This last day has been completely hideous! Even now that it's all over, my nerves jump and my scalp prickles at the very thought of it. I can still hear the screams of dying men and beasts, the shrill whistling of Ithaqua's man-carrying kites as they soared down upon the plateau out of raging skies, the blasts of the thunderbolts that turned the plateau's roof to an incredible inferno; and I can still smell the ozone reek of alien energies, the stench of living fear, the sordid stink of death. But let me tell you Ithaqua did not have it all his own way. And for all the plateau's losses the Wind-Walker strides by no means triumphant in Borea's skies this day. He licks an awful wound, and his warriors are scattered far and wide.

But I can't get Whitey out of my mind, poor Whitey, who will have no grave for there is nothing to bury. But, by God! – we shall raise to him a memorial where he died, a tower of stone on the very roof of the plateau, to overlook this whole demon-damned world forever.

And I'm sorry, Juanita; as yet you know nothing of all this, and here I rave like a man demented. Well, perhaps you will understand when I am finished.

It started within an hour of my last contact with you . . .

One minute the strangely hummocked white expanse, with all its frozen loot of the Motherworld of men, seemed empty of life, except about the totem ring and its central altar, where tents and shelters had been set up to house the army that Northan had gathered and disciplined for the Wind-Walker. The next moment the whole plain turned black! Shedding the white furs which until then had kept them hidden, the massed might of the Children of the Winds was revealed.

To think that a few moments earlier I had been wondering where all of Ithaqua's warriors had gone! Having watched them gathering for days, from far and wide, I had noticed that paradoxically there never seemed to be more than a few thousand of them visible at any one time. Now at last they showed themselves. Ten ranks deep, only a shoulder's width between them, forming a straight line that stretched for at least five miles across the wastes, I calculated that they numbered close to two hundred thousand. And these were only the foot soldiers!

Behind them, three deep and stretching in a line all of two miles long, in the next moment appeared the wolf-warriors. They too threw down their robes to reveal their great numbers, a move calculated to unnerve us. And certainly Ithaqua's army was an unnerving sight. Oh, the Wind-Walker was not playing games this time, neither him nor his new warlord, Northan.

Northan! My lips drew back from my teeth involuntarily as I thought of the treacherous hound, and almost as if I had once more thrown a challenge in his face, so the sails of the plateau's once-flagship filled out as it slipped anchor near the pyramid altar. My nails bit into the metal of my binoculars as I focused them on the ship

182

of Northan, thought at that distance the figures crowding her decks were tinier than ants and I could never have said for certain which one was he.

The ship rode out to the forefront of the army, gathering speed as it took up a central position, and now the army itself began to move, forming an arrowhead behind the ship. I could see the wolf-warriors spurring their huge mounts to advance through the ranks of the foot soldiers. As the wolves came, so the men on foot jumped up to cling to their great sides and be carried forward.

Bringing up the rear came great battle-sledges hauled by teams of lesser wolves, and these picked up the remaining foot soldiers. I kept my binoculars upon these battle-sledges and after a few seconds managed to obtain a better view of them. They were mounted with stout, pointed battering-rams.

Finally, behind all the others, Ithaqua's priests rode in their own sledges. Forming a backdrop to that awesome army of men and beasts, the Wind-Walker himself stood atop his frozen altar with massive arms folded and terrible eyes hooded as in deep, dark thoughts.

I put down my binoculars. The V-shaped formation could mean only one thing: a direct assault upon the plateau, concentrated upon a narrow front. And the battering-rams told me that the attack must come at the gates of the snow-ship keeps, which were all positioned along an uneven half-mile of the plateau's front.

Once through those heavy gates the wolf-warriors might well manage to breach one or more of the larger tunnels that led directly into the plateau's bowels, doubly fortified as they now were. I was sure that this was what Northan intended to do, and so issued my first orders. All of the runners were fluent in English, and no sooner had the first of my messengers darted away down the steep flights of stone steps with my instructions than the next was there, eager to receive my next command. I told all of them to

183

sit down and try to relax; orders would be issued as they were required.

That was when Charlie Tacomah entered from one of the two horizontal shafts that led back into the plateau. I appreciated his company and repeated for his benefit the orders I had given a few seconds earlier. He borrowed my binoculars, studied the advancing army and nodded.

'I think I would have done the same thing,' he said. 'It's a pity we had no time to build sufficient of our swinging weapons to completely block off the larger tunnels that enter from the keeps. They form our weakest points. Yes, I too would have sent more men there.' He paused, at length added, 'And what of our elite corps?'

'The snow-ships? I want to hold them back until Northan and his army are closer, then release them all at once. As I see it, Ithaqua is filling the sails of Northan's ship with just sufficient wind to blow him to the plateau along with the rest of the army. From here we are looking at them down a very slight slope, and in that we have an advantage. If we keep the snow-ships back until the last moment, then get Armandra to give them a push, they ought at least to be able to punch a couple of holes through that V-formation. After that –' I shook my head, frowning. 'If I had my way I wouldn't let them sail at all. Not only does it mean bringing Armandra into it, albeit indirectly, and not in any real sort of confrontation with the Wind-Walker – but I'm sure that it will be certain death for many of the lads who man the snow-ships.'

'They would not thank you for holding them back, Hank.'

'And will I thank myself for sending them out to die?'

'That has always been the lot of generals, and of war-lords.'

I nodded grimly, then took the binoculars back and put them to my eyes once more. Now Northan's army was a quarter of the way to the plateau, and already one or two stragglers could be seen stretching out to the rear. Northan's ship still rode slightly to the fore, and that must be the traitor himself in the prow, surrounded by his lieutenants. There were wolves aboard that ship too, massive white beasts that strained at their chains. An idea – a suspicion – came to me.

'Do you think it is possible,' I asked, 'that Northan intends to crash one of the gates with his ship, then release those great wolves to ravage along the tunnels? There are about three dozen of the beasts aboard, but I can see damn few handlers.'

'Wolves? Without handlers?' He took back the binoculars and a moment later said, 'You could well be right. They will be lean and hungry animals, those wolves.'

I turned to one of my runners. 'Go tell the crews of the snow-ships to be ready. The keep gates are to be opened. All are then to wait for new orders.'

As the runner hurried off I turned again to Charlie. 'It seems we'll have to deal with the ship of Northan first,' I said. 'But just in case he should manage to break into one of the keeps with those wolves of his –' I clapped the next boy in line on the shoulder. 'Go to Kota'na. I want twenty of his biggest, most powerful bears positioned in each of the keeps. The rest of them he is to use to their best advantage as soon as the fighting starts.'

Now Ithaqua's army had covered more than half the distance to the plateau and the tension was rapidly heightening. I began to pace the floor, then forced myself to sit down when I noticed the eyes of my runners upon me. Charlie opened his mouth to say something, and at that precise moment there came a swelling cry from the central snow-ship keep somewhere below and to the left of my position, a cry that was echoed almost immediately from the flanking keeps.

'Sil-ber-*hut-te! * Sil-ber-*hut-te!*'

Obviously the runner had passed on my message to the men of the snow-ships, and now they signalled their wholehearted approval. Something swelled up inside me as once more, in unison, the men of the snow-ships roared out their new battle cry. 'Sil-ber-*hut-te!* Sil-ber-*hut-te!*'

The swelling thing inside me burst in a flood of resolution. I stood up and said to my Indian friend, 'You keep the binoculars, Charlie. You'll need them if you're to command the battle. Those men out there are calling my name. They're not going to fight without me.'

'*No!*' came Armandra's almost hysterical, mental denial in my head. '*You shall not, for if you do – then I swear I will walk out now on the winds to fight my father. Aye, even knowing that he will snatch me up and take me away with him to alien worlds. Without you, man of the Motherworld, there would be nothing for me here on Borea. Do you hear me, Hank? You shall not give your life away!*'

'*But they call my name, and –*'

'*They draw upon your name for its strength. They invoke your passions, your power. Why should you go out to fight, Hank, when every man of the plateau will fight with your great strength and fervour? They know you are worthy of them, now let them prove that they are worthy of you. And remember, husband, we made a bargain. If you fight, then so do I.*'

'They are closer, Hank.' Charlie's voice snatched me back to the task at hand. 'What are you going to do?'

Still torn two ways but realizing there was nothing I could do about it, I said, 'Armandra leaves me no choice. I can't let her do battle with her father, so I must stay here and command from this position of safety. You stay with me, Charlie. Two heads are better than one.'

Out on the plain, less than two miles now from the foot of the plateau, the wolf-warrior army swept toward us, its arrowhead formation slightly less pronounced. Northan had lined up his vessel on the central snow-ship keep. I slapped my next runner on his back. 'Go tell the crews of the snow-ships to move out and position their craft along the front of the plateau.' I took up my pistol. There was one bullet left in its magazine. 'When they hear a loud report from this cave, they'll go straight out and cut through the advancing wolf-warriors. The two central ships will engage Northan's vessel and try to wreck it.'

'*Armandra*,' I continued telepathically, '*we will need a wind . . .*'

'*You shall have one. With luck it will take my father by surprise.*'

'This is it, Hank,' Charlie said breathlessly. 'Only a few seconds now.'

He had the binoculars to his eyes. 'You were right about those wolves on Northan's ship. They are huge, lean, ferocious animals. They look half-wild, barely trained and certainly starved.'

I spoke to yet another runner. 'Every man of the plateau should now be in position. I want the swinging weapons set in motion and the keep gates closed as soon as the ships are out. More of our bears are to be stationed just within the gates.'

As he raced away down one of the steep shafts I stepped over to the lip of the cave and looked down to where the snow-ships would soon be lining up. After only a minute or so they began to appear from the keeps, dragged by teams of men and bears. There were eleven of them, and as they lined up the eyes of all crew members turned up to me.

Now Northan's army was little more than a half-mile away and gaining speed. The sails of the traitor's ship belled out in front, drawing the vessel straight for the gates of the central keep. The rumble of that army swept up to me as I turned to look at Charlie Tacomah. I nodded my head and he grimly nodded back. Then I pointed my

187

weapon out over the white wastes and pulled the trigger for the last time. I said to the Woman of the Winds, '*Now we need that wind, Armandra.*'

'*You have it,*' she answered.

Flurries of ice particles swirled up all around the snow-ships and their great sails filled. They lurched forward, masts straining as the force of the wind Armandra had sent rapidly increased. And once more that massed cry came up to me as if from one vast throat: 'Sil-ber-*hut-te!* Sil-ber-*hut-te!*'

Down the shallow decline the ships sailed, their skis throwing up a silver spray, and now the wolf-warrior army also felt the wind sent by Armandra. Northan's ship visibly slowed and its sails seemed to slacken as the plateau's two central vessels bore down upon it. I had ordered that those ships engage Northan's craft; now I saw that they intended to ram him!

But if that fact was plain to me, it was equally obvious to the wolf-warriors. A battle sledge was hurriedly thrown into the path of the starboard vessel, and as its skis cut great swathes through wolves and men, so they ran into the bulky obstacle. A snapping of timbers as two of the skis were ripped away; then the screams of men and animals as the snow-ship toppled, crushing down upon the milling ranks of those around it, flinging its crew to the frozen ground where, miraculously unhurt, they quickly formed themselves and their bears into a savage fighting unit.

The other ship fared somewhat better. Its bird's-beak prow struck Northan's vessel a glancing blow that threw both ships a little starboard. As their decks passed each other, scraping together, men of the plateau leaped the gunwales to engage hand-to-hand with Northan's crew. Then I saw that indeed Charlie had been right about those wolves on Northan's ship; these were not wolves bred to be ridden as mounts, nor were they bulky for the hauling of heavy loads. They were lean and rangy killers!

And three or four of them had hurdled the rails between the passing ships and were now ravaging among the crew of the plateau's vessel, while their snarling brothers tore to pieces that brave raiding party aboard the ship of Northan. Ah, but in a few moments more the bears of the plateau's ship had turned on the attacking wolves to throw their mangled bodies from the swaying deck. The ship sailed on, leaving in its wake a crushed and bloody swath.

There were ten such swaths, red on the white plain as those heroic vessels ploughed through the wolf-warrior ranks; ten one instant, but in the next only seven as three more of the great ships were wrecked upon battle-sledge reefs. And as I watched, two more, steering wildly from their courses to pick up survivors, were flung onto their sides; in a moment only five ships remained and the plain was a tumult of fighting men and animals.

But no! Those brave men of the surviving snow-ships could not see their brothers go down alone against such odds. As their vessels slowed and stopped, brought to a halt by the sheer weight of shattered flesh and bone that clogged their massive skis, so their crews lowered the gangplanks and rushed down them onto the plain.

At last the snow-ships stood empty, while on the plain about them the Children of the Winds turned inwards on the now desperately battling, stranded crews. I turned my eyes away as that wolf-warrior tide washed over them, drowned them as a wave covers pebbles on a beach, then seethed forward again in triumph.

Gone, all those brave men gone. They had sailed out to their deaths with my name on their lips. But their lives were not wasted, for the snow was red beneath that surging tide of wolf-warriors, red with the blood of hundreds of men and wolves crushed beneath the skis, and certainly in the hand-to-hand fighting the plateau's braves had not given their lives cheaply.

Meanwhile Northan's ship, thrown off course by the glancing collision, had come about in a tight circle. Now, heedless of the scrambling men and beasts too slow to clear a path for him, the traitor returned his vessel to its previous course. Straight for the central keep gates its beaked prow was aimed, the breath of Ithaqua in its sails, and the sea of men and wolves before it parted in frantic haste as it sped to its target.

Would Northan see the star-stone where Tracy had nailed it to the centre of the great gate? Would it deter him? I had had concentric red circles painted around all such protective stars, to draw the eyes of the attacking army and fill them with dread. Surely Northan would see the star-stone. I took my binoculars back from Charlie and, with hands I could scarcely control, refocused upon Northan's ship.

There stood the ex-warlord upon the raised deck of the prow, eyes slitted and staring straight ahead, lips drawn back in a snarl. He would breach that gate if it was the last act he ever performed, and to hell with whatever awaited him on the other side!

Below me where I stood at the very lip of the cave, the forward part of the central keep and its gates were just visible. In that moment I looked down at a steep angle upon the ship of Northan. And at the same time, with something less than twice the length of his ship between him and the gates, finally Northan spotted the star-stone within its painted circles. He saw it and knew it to be genuine. I still had him in my binoculars when that happened, and the effect upon him was dramatic!

The snarl slid like butter from his face. He gabbled frenzied orders, motioned wildly with spastic arms, then hung on tight to the rail of the prow. Two of his lieutenants standing with him threw up their arms before their faces as they, too, spotted the star-stone. Then the ship slewed crazily as its crew-finally interpreted and acted upon Northan's orders. Chunks of ice flew up from the skis of his ship as they bit into the frozen surface.

Broadside, the traitor's vessel slammed splinteringly into the gate.

2

Battle for the Plateau

(Recorded through the Medium of Juanita Alvarez)

As Northan's snow-ship came to a shuddering halt at the splintered gates of the central keep, a clattering and shouting reached me from the almost vertical shafts. From closer at hand there came a savage howl as, turning, I barely found time to throw myself to one side. A hurled spear flashed past me and out through the open mouth of the cave.

Intent upon Northan's activities, I had given little thought to what was happening with the rest of the plateau. I had seen the wolf-warrior tide surging about the foot of our massive refuge; now it was made perfectly plain to me that one or more of the lesser tunnels had been breached. An Eskimo warrior, wearing on his back, shoulders and head the pelt and snarling visage of a wolf, stood astride the broken body of a youthful runner at the head of one of the steep shafts. Pulling out a long knife from his belt he stepped menacingly into the cave.

Just inside the cave, hidden from the Eskimo by a wall-like bulge of rock, Charlie Tacomah had seen the flight of the spear. He remained silent and as the Eskimo came forward swung his handaxe full in the intruder's face. The spine of that hideous weapon drove to its hilt in the fatally surprised Eskimo's forehead, splitting his skull open like a ripe melon and sending him toppling back and out of sight down the vertiginous steps. He gave a single gurgling shriek as he went.

Before I could thank Charlie, a guardsman wearing Armandra's royal insignia appeared from that same shaft.

How he had avoided being knocked from the steps by the Eskimo's falling body I was unable to think. Covered with blood – which clearly was not his own – the man bowed as he pantingly entered. Quickly he addressed me in his own tongue, which Charlie roughly translated:

'Three of the tunnels have been entered and a number of men and wolves are loose within the plateau. The rear parties and guardsmen are tracking them down. One of them has already surrendered himself and has volunteered important information. He was one of Northan's men originally and fled the plateau only under extreme pressure from the warlord. Northan's intention is to wreck the plateau and carry off both Tracy and Armandra. Even if he cannot take the plateau, he must not return without the women. Ithaqua will not allow Northan to fail him.'

A terrible foreboding suddenly gripped me. 'Charlie, take over.' I tossed him the binoculars as I ran past the bloodied guardsman and swerved into a shaft that led into the plateau's labyrinths. 'I have to get to Tracy. She's with Jimmy Franklin, and if the wolf-warriors have managed to get men this far into the plateau so quickly I'm taking no chances!'

I need not have worried. As I arrived at the head of a flight of stairs that reached down to the lower levels and the open cave where Jimmy had set up his catapult, he and my sister were just appearing from below. They were accompanied by four massive Eskimo guardsmen. Tracy was dishevelled and Jimmy had bruises and a few cuts, but aside from a superficial roughing-up neither of them seemed seriously hurt.

Relief flooded my being at the sight of Tracy's shaky but reassuring smile. 'I must be crazy,' I told Jimmy, 'to let you set up that sling of yours so close to the foot of the plateau. What happened?'

'No one's fault, Hank,' he answered. 'I guess we just underestimated the enemy's penetration power. A pair of wolf-warriors made it up to our cave.' He looked grim as he added, 'They weren't so hard, though – not after they saw Tracy's pile of star-stones. And I know just how they felt. I was pretty terrified of those stones myself.'

Excitement suddenly filled his voice. 'You should have seen it, Hank. When we started hurling the stones at Ithaqua's army – what a frenzy and a scattering! Anyway, during the scramble the catapult was wrecked, then I got one of the intruders with his own spear. But by God – spears and tomahawks are no match for star-stones! While I was occupied with my man the other one tried to get behind me. Tracy managed to hit him with a stone. It seemed to stick in him and burn there. His side seemed to roast away!'

'Oh, Jimmy, don't!' Tracy cried, the tremulous smile dropping instantly from her face. She looked suddenly very small, pale and frightened. Only her tremendous courage was keeping her going.

'A couple of seconds after that,' Jimmy finished off, 'these fellows arrived – just too late to give us a hand. They told us it wouldn't be safe for a while in the lower levels. There are about a hundred enemy warriors loose down there, not to mention some two dozen wolves.'

'That many!' I gasped. 'Look, you'd better follow me to Armandra. Two of the guardsmen will stay with you, in case you come up against trouble along the way. The other two can go and help Charlie Tacomah. He's running the show now. I have to get a move on. And look after Tracy, Jimmy. I happen to know that Northan has plans to kidnap her. He's after Armandra, too. I'll see you both later.'

No sooner had I left them, climbing in a spiral toward the uppermost levels, then I sensed Armandra's mental presence. I opened my mind and she said, 'Hank, what is happening?'

'There are wolf-warriors in the plateau, I don't know how many. The guardsmen and rear parties are hunting them

194

down but you may be in danger, Armandra. Northan means to take you back to Ithaqua, and Tracy with you. Tracy is safe enough for now, but what about you?'

'There are eight guardsmen within hailing distance, plus Kasna'chi and Gosan-ha. All are sworn to protect me with their lives.'

'You should have ten,' I told her.

She answered, *'I sent two of them away with their bears. I ordered them to the snow-ship keeps, to the side of Kota'na, Oontawa's man.'*

'Good,' I said. *'I'm sure there's a lot more of your mother's nature in you than you suspect, Armandra. Anyway, I'm on my way to you. I've left Charlie Tacomah in command; he will make a better job of it than I could. Right now I'm wondering what tricks Northan and Ithaqua have up their sleeves.'*

With that thought another occurred to me: the plateau had a couple of tricks of its own. By now the wolf-warriors should be attacking in a frustrated crush all along the face of the plateau. I hoped the holes they had already found in our defences had by now been blocked. All being well, Charlie Tacomah should have ordered the pouring of the burning oil down upon the heads of the invaders. The plateau's mineral oil reserves had provided a defensive device of hideous potency.

Armandra plucked the thought out of my head.

'Yes, I have been to the balcony. The foot of the plateau is a sea of fire. The Children of the Winds are dying by the hundreds.' No trace of pleasure showed in her thoughts. Alien though her anger might be, her compassion was warm and human.

'Go back to the balcony,' I told her. *'I'll meet you there. I want to see how things are going.'*

'Things seem to be going well for us indeed. But war is – terrible. The only thing in it that gives me pleasure is the thought of my father at this very moment. He must

195

*be beside himself with rage! I will go now to the balcony.
Hank?'*

'Yes?'

'Take care.'

Two-thirds of the way to my destination the sounds of
a chase reached me. I slowed to a halt and as I stood there
trying to control my breathing and listening in the light of
many flickering flambeaux, it soon became apparent that
the sounds of flight and pursuit were coming closer. In a
few seconds more three wolf-warriors, clinging to the sides
of one great wolf, burst from the mouth of a horizontal
tunnel.

They saw me. As they dropped from the wolf's sides like
ticks from an infested dog, one of them spoke to the beast.
It sprang at me, its massive muzzle thrusting forward. I
had a spear but no time to throw it. I leaned back on the
shaft of the weapon until its hilt found a purchase against
the uneven floor, bracing it against the wolf's spring. The
great beast impaled itself on the spear, knocking me aside
and wrenching the weapon from my hands.

While the wolf howled out its life in agony on the floor,
the three warriors came at me in a rush. Weaponless, I
threw myself up a flight of steps, turning to kick the fastest
of my pursuers full in the face. He fell from the steps with
a scream and crashed to the stone floor head first.

I made to climb higher and one of the remaining warriors threw himself after me. He grabbed my foot, causing
me to lose my balance and fall between him and his
companion. On my back, I managed to catch the wrist
of one of my attackers as he aimed his tomahawk at my
face, and while I briefly wrestled with him on the steps
I wondered why the other man made no attempt to help
his colleague.

Then as finally I overcame my attacker and throttled
him with the haft of his own weapon, I saw why his friend
had not helped him. The last of the three invaders was

tottering down the steps, uselessly tugging at a spear that transfixed him. A second flashing spear pierced him as I watched, hurling him from the steps.

Then two of the plateau's guardsmen hurried up to me while five more positioned themselves at the mouths of the gallery's tunnels. 'Are you all right, Lord?' one of my rescuers, a strapping young Viking, asked as I climbed to my feet.

'My thanks for your timely intervention,' I answered. 'Yes, I'm unhurt. But how goes it now? How many more of Northan's warriors lurk in the plateau's caves and tunnels?'

'Perhaps a dozen of them,' he answered, 'but they, too, will soon be hunted down.'

'And their wolves?'

'Few remain, Lord.'

This man seemed well informed; he had obviously been in a position to follow the course of events closely. 'What about the plateau's losses?'

'The snow-ships and their crews are lost.'

'I know,' I answered. 'I saw it. They were brave men.'

'Within the plateau, when the first wolf-warriors found a way in, we lost some men and bears. A man for a man, a bear for two wolves, perhaps. Now that they can no longer get in –'

'I have no time now for talk,' I cut him off, 'but you have made my mind easier. Do not stop, but keep on searching the wolf-warriors out. Tell any others of the plateau's men you may meet the same thing. Now I go to Armandra.'

And as I continued on my way, as if invoked by my mentioning her name, Armandra's mental voice came to me again: *'I am at the balcony, Hank. Is anything wrong?'*

'A bit of a scuffle,' I answered. *'Don't worry, nothing came of it.'*

'The wolf-warrior hordes have pulled back from the foot of the plateau,' she informed me, *'out of the way of the*

blazing oil. But it seems to me that Ithaqua's priests are up to some trickery.'

'*I'll be with you in a minute or so,*' I said, entering the final gallery and crossing it to the tunnel with the lightning-flash symbol. And there I was brought up short in sheerest shock and terror. Terror not for myself, for Armandra. There, sprawled in attitudes of grisly death, lay three of my woman's guardsmen – bear, too, its spilled entrails still steaming – and the bodies of four wolf-warriors and a wolf.

Tired as I was from my race against gravity and time, my heels grew wings as I threw myself down the perimeter corridor and finally turned into the jutting balcony with its widely spaced bars. And there, his back to me, tomahawk raised to deliver a stunning blow, an Indian in the matted apparel of a wolf-warrior furtively crouched.

Beyond him, ignorant of his presence, Armandra stood at the bars, staring down at the plain where the Children of the Winds milled in confusion and frustration; but as I entered in a rush they both turned. She saw him even as he saw me, and as he leaped to meet me she cried out, '*No!*'

His reactions were quick and I was tired. His weapon caught me a glancing blow on the head that sent me dazed to my knees. Up went his tomahawk again and his wild cry was one of certain victory – cut short in strangled amazement!

He was whirled off his feet, thrust aloft and spread-eagled in midair by centrifugal force as his body spun even faster in mad currents of air. The suddenly howling wind that filled the balcony snatched at my hair, hurled me aside, slammed the shrieking wolf-warrior time and again against the uneven surface of the ceiling, finally shot him headlong, with a snapping of bones, out through the bars and away into empty abysses of icy air.

And slowly the sentient hair fell back upon her head and her blazing crimson eyes dulled as Armandra ran to me sobbing, a woman once more, where only seconds earlier an elemental of the air had commanded familiar winds!

I held her tight and for the moment there was no war in progress, no shadow over Borea. Then I became angry.

'Where are the rest of your guardsmen? I saw only three of them, all dead, back along the perimeter tunnel – what of the rest?'

'Three of my men, dead?'

'They died to stop this man and his brothers reaching you – and they almost died in vain.'

'I sent the others away,' she admitted, leading me over to the bars of the balcony. 'They wanted to join in the fighting and I felt capable of fending for my –'

'Oh, did you?' I cut her off. 'And if I had not come along when I did?'

'But you *did* come, Hank. Now come, we have no time for quarrelling. Look down there. What do you make of that?'

I took hold of the bars and looked out. The wolf-warrior army had pulled back to a distance of about one hundred and fifty yards from the foot of the plateau. There against the white of the plain they formed a deep dark band that stretched away and around the curving protective walls of rock to both sides. Between them and the fortified tunnels and keeps an ocean of fire, its warmth reaching up to me even at this height, blazed and roared. At first I could not see what was causing Armandra's concern, then I saw that the wolf-warriors were opening up to leave clear paths through their ranks from the rear to the front. They were making way for something. But what?

'My father's so-called "priests," see?' Armandra said, pointing. 'There, at the rear of the army. And now I know what they are about.'

'Yes, I've seen them cavorting like that before,' I agreed. 'Then they were calling up those tornadoes of theirs, working their devilish magic through your father.'

'That is exactly what they are doing now,' she said. 'See? And once they have called up their snow-devils they will throw them into the fire and smother it. And then –'

'Then?'

She turned to look at me with wide, unflinching eyes. 'Then they will hurl those whirligigs at the tunnel entrances, the keep gates. They will drive them deep into the plateau, and the wolf-warriors will follow behind!'

'Armandra, I –'

'I have promised not to fight my father, Hank, but those – *creatures* of his, his "priests" – they must be stopped!'

'If you interfere, it may draw Ithaqua into the battle.'

'And if I don't, the plateau is lost anyway.'

Down below six spinning tops had appeared, each with its own capering master behind it, urging it on. Six alien whirlwinds that grew up rapidly out of the frozen plain and moved threateningly forward, roaring along the paths cleared by the wolf-warriors, entering and obscuring in clouds of steam and smoke the field of blazing oil fires.

Armandra was right and I knew it. In another moment Ithaqua's priests would hurl those spinning pillars directly at the keeps and major tunnel entrances. They would wipe the tunnels clean of men and bears in seconds. The swinging engines that carried the star-stones might be safe enough, Ithaqua's familiar winds and powers were restricted by his own limitations. But not all of the tunnels were so well protected, and only the actual gates of the keeps carried those symbols of Eld. To simply allow these priests of the Wind-Walker to use their tools of an alien science as they desired would be suicidal.

'Armandra,' I told her, 'do whatever must be done.'

From beside me, so close that I felt her breath fanning my cheek as she spoke, and in a tone that called up visions of unknown star-voids, she said, 'It is already begun!'

I glanced at her and felt the hair of my neck prickle at the sight of that strange pink flush that spread outwards from the closed eyes to fill her pale face. I stepped quickly back as her hair began to rise up in undulating coils above her head and the white fur smock she wore stirred with weird life.

Gone again was the woman I loved, gone in a matter of seconds to make way for this child of Ithaqua, whose arms now reached up to beckon to the suddenly agitated sky. High above, grey clouds turned black, then blue, boiling in an instant and flashing with trapped energies. A continuous rumbling filled the pregnant air.

The fine bones of Armandra's head and neck showed redly through luminous flesh, a grinning skull of death. Her eyes opened; beams of blinding ruby radiance shot forth to the pulsating sky; she made stabbing motions with her hands, which were curved downward now like the heads of swans.

And then I was sent staggering back from the bars, away from the vicious rain of red lightning that lashed down in staccato precision from the sky to the plain below! I did not see those deadly white funnels destroyed – saw nothing of the carnage among the massed ranks of the wolf-warriors when, finished with the sundered torna-does, Armandra simply rained her devastating energies down upon flesh and blood. I was told of it later, and then I was glad I had not seen it.

No, I saw nothing; nor, deafened from the first hellish salvo, did I hear anything, for which I am also grateful. And even when it was done, several minutes elapsed before I was able to perceive anything but the scarlet blaze burning on my retinas and the pounding of blood in my nearly ruptured eardrums.

Armandra lay huddled beside the bars, sobbing and momentarily spent. Again her terrific anger had vented itself uncontrollably, and again the human side of her nature was betrayed. I went dazedly forward to comfort her but then, as my eyes inadvertently looked down upon the plain, I froze in awed disbelief. Where an army had massed in premature triumph, a demoralized rabble now moved in blind, crippled agony.

Great black smoking craters littered the plain all along the front of the plateau, as if a squadron of bombers had unloaded their bomb bays there. Where the priests had capered to the rear, now a gutted trench lay straight as the furrow of a giant's plow in the icy ground. And in the wake of Armandra's inferno of lunatic lightnings, at last there sprang up a mournful wind that caught up the billowing smoke and steam to lay it like a veil across the whole scene, as if to hide the horror there.

Now, cradling the Woman of the Winds in my arms and rocking her, I heard drifting up to me a thousand amazed cries of utter disbelief and nameless horror from the survivors of that destroyed army. And rising above those cries came the lustful, reverberating battle cry of the plateau's fighting men:

'Sil-ber-*hut-te!* Sil-ber-*hut-te!*'

For a moment I cursed aloud, wildly and blasphemously. God, no! I would not have my name as a seal upon *that* – upon the carnage Armandra's blind fury had wrought. But then I was amazed to see that even now the remaining wolf-warriors, who still far outnumbered the men of the plateau, were rallying to the sort of battle they could understand.

And once more I felt my heart surge within me as out from the base of the plateau, from its tunnels and keeps, rushed the authors of that concerted battle cry, unleashed at last by Charlie Tacomah to earn their honour on a field of bloodied snow and ice!

3

War of the Winds

(Recorded through the Medium of Juanita Alvarez)

No sooner was the battle joined than my attention was distracted from it by footfalls sounding in the perimeter tunnel. One of the guardsmen I had left with Jimmy and Tracy hurried into view. He gave a cry of relief when he found us unharmed; he had passed the bodies of his colleagues at the entrance to the tunnel.

Now he composed himself, bowed first to Armandra and then turned to me. 'Lord, your sister, and your friend have gone to the roof of the plateau to view the fighting. They bade me come and tell you.'

I nodded. 'And your partner – did he go with them?'

'Yes, Lord.'

'Then you had better follow them. Stay with them until this is all over.'

He bowed again to me and again to Armandra, then hurried back the way he had come.

'If they wish to view the fighting,' Armandra said when he had gone, 'there are few better places from which to do so than here.'

'Perhaps they were seeking Whitey. The three of them have grown very close.'

'Whitey,' she mused, 'whose powers have deserted him. Is it a dark omen, I wonder?'

'It's a disadvantage, certainly, but I wouldn't consider it a dark omen. On the contrary, things are going very well. See, despite the odds your people are fighting an inspired battle. They are making a shambles of Ithaqua's army.'

'They are *our* people, Hank, yours and mine. And they

203

will be victorious because my father's wolf-warriors are demoralized. I have crippled them.' She stared for a few seconds at the milling scene below, then lifted her eyes to the distant pyramid altar of ice and heterogeneous 'trophies'. I followed her gaze as her eyes widened – and then we gasped in unison.

The Wind-Walker was raging, swelling out; his arms were lifted in a threatening attitude; his carmine eyes were blazing in his bloating face. In another moment he had stepped from his altar to stride aloft, and he was coming straight for the plateau!

'They have failed him,' Armandra gasped. 'The Children of the Winds have failed him yet again. Now he will seek vengeance upon the plateau – and upon his own men!'

'But how can he strike us?' I protested. 'The plateau is safeguarded by the star-stones.'

'Those star-stones of the Elder Gods!' she passionately cried. 'I loathe and abhor the things and the gloom they cast over the plateau and its people.'

'They are a symbol of benign power in the plateau,' I argued, 'and without them all would long ago have been lost.'

'A benign symbol, yes,' she answered, 'like the crucifix in the Motherworld. Don't you see, Hank, that all great symbols of power are horrific in their way?'

At the time I didn't give it a lot of thought, but now that I've thought about it I can see what she meant. Certainly the star-stone is benign to anyone not contaminated by Ithaqua or his hideous brothers of the Cthulhu Cycle. Of course the crucifix is a symbol of goodness, despite the fact that it is a model of a most terrible torture machine. The swastika too was an emblem of life, luck and power long before it became the outline of horror. What more innocuous than the hammer and sickle; tools of everyday life and labour?

'But look,' she said, 'perhaps you are right that my father is helpless to harm us. See, he hesitates.'

High above his totem temple the Wind-Walker hung motionless in the sky, his evil eyes glaring at the plateau. I knew that he saw – or felt – the power of the star-stones, those same stones which had held him so long impotent, and I knew that they repulsed him as surely as like magnetic poles repel each other.

'What is he doing?' I asked, as he commenced upward sweeping motions with monstrously bloated arms.

'He calls a wind,' she answered, frowning. 'But to what purpose, for surely no energies of his devising may strike us now?'

'Look!' I exclaimed. 'Those dots on the plain, black dots rising into the air, what are they?'

Rapidly the things I referred to climbed into the sky and were blown forward ahead of the Wind-Walker as he recommenced his striding toward the plateau, and a moment later I believed I knew what they were.

'Kites!' Armandra cried, confirming my own opinion. 'Kites shaped like bats that fly on my father's breath. And they carry men.'

'Man-carrying kites!' I gasped. 'But that must mean that he intends to land them –'

'On the roof,' she finished for me.

Then her eyes went very wide. 'Hank, I think it would have been better if Tracy and Jimmy had come here to us instead of going to the roof!'

'Oh my God!' I whispered, instinctively turning from her, heading for the perimeter tunnel.

She called out after me, 'Hank, wait!'

I came to a hesitant halt, half turned. 'I have to get them off the roof, out of harm's way.'

'If you go up there,' she said breathlessly, 'you will have to fight. See, already my father's man-kites approach. And if you fight. . . .' She shook her head wildly, as if shaking off the dark shapes of nightmare. 'I must not lose you now, man of Earth.'

'My sister and my friends, Armandra,' I quickly answered. 'I have no choice. I could never live with myself.' Then, wasting no more time, I ran from the balcony.

In my mind, before I could shut her out, she cried after me: *'Hank! Hank! Our bargain!'*

I knew that from the gallery at the far end of the primeter corridor a long flight of steps wound their way up to the roof; it should take me no more than two or three minutes to get up there. I raced along the corridor, started up the winding steps, taking them in threes, and as I went I gave credit to the evil intelligence that was Ithaqua.

He had known the weakest spot in the plateau's defences all along; the roof, where only a handful of men, few of them warriors, kept wary watch over the white wastes. Well, I was sure of one thing at least. No matter how many of his kites Ithaqua hurled at the plateau, no matter how heavy the odds, those watchers on the roof would stand and fight to the end.

Only four passageways in all led up to the flat, ruggedly stark roof, four orifices opening into the grey light of Borea. All four were spaced out across the roof's surface, the only accesses. What if Tracy and the others had been cut off from them? These and similar thoughts ran circles in my mind as I flew up the last few steps. In fact I must have taken well under the three minutes I had allowed myself, but it seemed as though half an hour had elapsed before finally I stood panting out in the open air, where the wind rushed over the slippery stone in furious blasts.

I paused briefly to assess the situation and get my breath back. Apart from the presence of a number of kite-men, there was something very wrong with the sight that now met my eyes – something which was soon to become plain to me.

I picked out the figures of Tracy, Jimmy and Whitey

almost immediately; they were fighting with those of Ithaqua's raiders who had already effected landings. With them were about a dozen watchmen, also caught unaware by the aerial attack.

They were not together in a group. Tracy was the most distant from me; about eighty yards separated us. She held up one of her star-stones before her, a threat to any of the Wind-Walker's men who might attempt to get too close. She had found this stone still on its chain where Northan's dupe had left it. The other one was lost, gone forever in some dark crevice in the forbidden tunnel. Tracy had not yet seen me. She appeared to be trying to make her way to Jimmy. I called out to her but my shout was lost in a frenzy of winds.

Jimmy was at the forward edge of the plateau, where waist-high battlements faced out across the white waste. As I saw him he was in the act of spearing one of the raiders who was just attempting a landing. Having killed his man with a single thrust, Jimmy toppled him from the roof along with his kite.

Whitey was the closest to me. Flanked by two of the watchmen, who fought equally furiously, he was battling like a madman to hold off a handful of the invaders. There were fifteen of us in all, against about the same number of kite-men, but more of the latter were landing all the time. One thing was heartening at least: for the moment Ithaqua stood away.

Dark and bloated against the grey skies, ten times taller than a tall man, the monster trod the air half a mile from the plateau's roof almost as a swimmer treads water. With his eyes blazing avidly and his arms half reaching forward, he formed the most fantastic part of the whole scene. I knew that he noted every detail of the situation, but that as eager as he was to destroy the plateau and steal back his daughter – and take Tracy, too, for his monstrous purposes – still the star-stones held him at bay.

The star-stones! Now I knew what had bothered me about the scene on the roof. Ithaqua's raiders were not trying to break into the plateau, they were there simply to clear the way for their master. He had sent them to destroy the great protective star that my sister had traced with star-stones on the plateau's roof! With that out of the way, Ithaqua would be able to completely command the roof and land as many of his aerial warriors upon it as he could muster.

And now, out there on the wings of the wind, I could see that there were *hundreds* of the kites. The brilliance of the Wind-Walker's stratagem was obvious. Ninety-five per cent of the plateau's soldiery were engaged in the battle down below, and the rest of the able-bodied men were at their posts deep down in the rocky labyrinths. Reinforcements would doubtless come, but would they be in time?

But no, my reasoning was way off – I must be wrong! The Children of the Winds couldn't possibly have been sent to get rid of the star-stones. They were as helpless against them as Ithaqua himself!

All of these things rushed through my mind as I surveyed the roof. Then I started to run toward Tracy, slowing for a second to snatch up a tomahawk from beside a dead kite-man. As I went I called her name again, and this time she heard me. That was a wonder, for above the howling of the wind, at precisely the same time that I called her, there came a shrieking like none I had ever heard before. It was the sound of a soul in torment, a banshee howling that froze my unnaturally chilled blood even further, causing me to seek wide-eyed for its source.

And when I found that source I knew that I had been right after all, and that the fear Ithaqua inspired in his 'children' was absolute.

One of the kite-men was tearing at a star-stone where it was fastened to the battlements. The flesh was visibly blackening on his hands as he scrabbled frenziedly to tear the stone loose. His screams did not stop for a single moment but grew shriller still as his fingers began to fall off. Finally he tore the stone free and clutched it to his chest, then gave the most hideous scream of all as black smoke poured out from him. He tottered for a moment, then, as the stench of his burning reached me on the rushing wind, crumbled like rotting wood and fell from the battlements.

Suddenly the wind increased, blowing especially from that region of the roof now unprotected by the stone sigil of Eld, and at the same time I noted shrieks of mortal terror and horror springing up from four other distinct points all around the rim of the plateau. Heedless of their fatal torment – which must have been the ultimate in physical and psychic agony – Ithaqua's aerial suicide squadron was proceeding with its task of clearing the roof. And as the star-stones were removed one by one, the Wind-Walker himself came closer, suspended in the sky.

I had not quite reached Tracy when two kite-men, freshly free of the harnesses of their aircraft, sprang at her. Their weapons were still in their belts and it was plain that their task was to render her helpless and somehow bear her away. I threw my weapon just as one of them went to strike her with his clenched fist. As she ducked his blow and swung her star-stone on its chain full in his face, my tomahawk bit into his side. It is possible that he didn't even feel the bite of my weapon for the agony of Tracy's. His face caved in, black and ruined, and he went down as though a truck had hit him. The second man turned toward me but was thrown down by the force of my rush. As he started to rise I kicked him in the throat as hard as I could. Tracy freed her star-stone from the mess of the first man's face, and as I backed hastily away she began to be sick.

Looking about me I saw that almost all of the invaders had been dealt with, killed and swept from the roof as they had gone about their task of clearing its surface of star-stones. Nevertheless, they seemed to have successfully completed that task. There came a weird, shrill whistling, emanating from the hundreds of batlike shapes that still hung in the sky between the plateau's roof and the swollen figure of the Snow-Thing. The kites were soaring forward, the wind whistling its demon song in their frames of poles and stretched hides. Now Ithaqua could take possession of the roof, land the rest of his airborne forces and invade the plateau.

'Tracy!' I yelled in her ear. 'Get below. I want everyone off the roof. We'll be outnumbered in no time at all and Ithaqua himself may even make a landing here.' I pointed her in the direction of the tunnel I had used and gave her a gentle push. She started to slip and stumble away from me, barely keeping her feet as the wind's strength rapidly increased.

Having seen her on her way to safety, I signalled to Whitey, Jimmy and the remaining handful of watchmen that they, too, should get below where they could better defend the four entrances. Seeing that they understood my signals, I turned to follow Tracy and was greeted by a sight that shocked me rigid. She had fallen and was sliding in the wind across the icy surface of the roof. Ithaqua had seen her and was moving after her!

He came forward and poised himself above the rim of the plateau, his vast feet seeking purchase on the battlements. From side to side his great bloated head went, slitted star-eyes taking in every detail of what was happening. They found Tracy again and stayed upon her where she finally slid to a halt against a projection of rock. Then the Wind-Walker stepped down onto the roof and reached for her with a massive hand. Immediately she held up her star-stone against his approach . . .

Slits of burning evil opened huge and round as the horror stepped hastily back and lifted into the air. Rage filled every line of his nightmare form. He trembled with an inner fury that swelled him out more hugely yet, completely distorting his already grotesque proportions, then he abruptly thrust up a hand to the clouds that raced across the sky.

I knew instinctively what he was about. While his alien powers could not work *directly* against my sister as long as she held that star-stone, he could use them *indirectly* in a purely physical attack, and now he would simply kill her out of hand and be done with it. I tried to go after her, only to be blown off my feet and sent slithering helplessly across the roof. Fighting to find a hold on the slippery surface, I managed to keep my eyes on Ithaqua and saw him pluck a great ball of ice out of the clouds. I saw his face convulse insanely as he hurled his missile at the roof.

I thought then that Tracy was done for, but I had reckoned without Jimmy Franklin. Tracy was my sister, yes, and I loved her, but Jimmy's love was that of a man for his woman. He fought his way to where she crouched against the outcrop of rock, and dragged her behind it at the very instant that Ithaqua released his ice-bomb. Now that bomb burst like a massive grenade where she had crouched a second earlier, but in the protective lee of the great rock, she and Jimmy were unharmed.

Since she was no longer visible to Ithaqua after the flying shards of ice dispersed, perhaps the monster thought her dead. I think it must have been so, for apparently without another thought for her he turned his attention to me.

And if horror can grin, now this monster grinned; if evil can express delight, Ithaqua was delighted.

Sliding helplessly before the howling wind, flat on my back and scrabbling at the icy stone beneath me, I felt his mind probe mine. Before I could shut him out he said something to me, showed me alien pictures, made

211

me understand. It was no sort of telepathic transmission that I could ever hope to explain, not even to another telepath, and yet I understood its meaning:

'*So. You are that man of Earth who dared set himself against me. That same one who hurls insults with his mind and threatens with powers of Eld. You are the one who would take the very seed of my being for your own, to make a mere mortal of her. You are nothing, man of Earth, and nothing you shall remain.*'

He reached one arm to the sky and pointed his other hand at me. I saw strange energies forming in the clouds, a flickering radiance that ran down his extended arm to his body and turned its barely manlike outline to an ever-changing display of crimson and golden traceries of light. In another instant that electrical nightmare would leap from his outstretched finger to me, and I would cease to be.

'*Father!*' There came a pure, bell-like resonance in my mind, a call which I heard even though it was not directed at me. '*Ithaqua – you will not take what is mine!*'

Unable to face the crackling holocaust that I knew was soon to come, I had closed my eyes. Now I opened them and lifted my head from the frozen stone surface. Of a number of things that were happening, the most important to me was that Ithaqua had partly turned away from me to face the forward rim of the plateau where now, floating slowly into view, the form of Armandra rose up. With her appearance the wind seemed abruptly to die away, to crouch down into itself and back off like a scolded dog.

'*Armandra,*' I said to her, reaching beyond the alien mask she wore to the sane and human side of her nature, '*I thank you for my life – but not at the expense of your own!*'

'*Do not distract me, Hank. All is not lost, not yet, but I need my concentration.*' To think that those mental tones of purest gold had come from the female horror that rode

212

the wind above the rim of the plateau! Her hair was floating in fiery, undulating waves over her head; her face was a death-mask. In that skull-like face, carmine pits of hell blazed in supernatural fury to match her father's own. She was tiny, compared to him, but her hatred and anger were great.

As she rose higher above the battlements, streams of guardsmen and warriors began to rush from the four exits. Pouring out onto the roof, they looked much fiercer than I ever remembered seeing them before, and I believed I knew why. One way or the other this was to be the final scene, and they knew it. They were here to lay down their lives for their princess, their world. At last they had been given an opportunity to fight, these men who had formed the rear parties, and they had arrived barely in time. Now great hordes of Ithaqua's kite-men were landing all about the roof, freeing themselves from their harnesses, moving into battle positions.

While all this was happening, I was almost unable to believe that somehow I had been spared. I came back to life, and my heart began to beat a little more freely as I saw that those energies Ithaqua had almost hurled at me were dying away, that the traceries of fire no longer permeated his dark form. He had apparently forgotten all about me; now he held out his bloated arms to Armandra in an attitude which, despite his completely alien nature, was almost humanly imploring. In answer she raised one pale arm above her head and rotated her hand, as if to spin the sky upon her fingers. And indeed the clouds immediately above her began to turn with her hand.

Undaunted, Ithaqua stepped closer, his monstrous feet treading air as he narrowed the gap separating him from his daughter. But this was no gap of merely physical dimensions. It was unbridgeable in anything other than the crudest physical sense. She floated back away from him, glowing with a scarlet flush, and faster yet her arm

213

twirled above her head. Then, without warning, she lowered her hand to a forward, horizontal position and jabbed it viciously in her hideous father's direction.

From the whirling clouds directly above her, lightning at once struck, branching into a blinding fork that speared at Ithaqua's eyes. He never moved, but stood unblinking and still as a hawk on the wind. Only those hellish orbs of his changed; they momentarily flared brighter as twin tongues of lightning were quenched in them. He had not even bothered to ward off Armandra's initial attack; what is the blow of a child to a man full grown? Ah, but that first blow of hers had opened up floodgates of accumulated loathing.

Now she stabbed at her father again and again, her hand like the tongue of some venomous reptile, invoking powers I had once believed to belong to nature alone. Lightning flashed in an almost continuous stream from the clouds to Ithaqua's form, filling him with blue and white fire. Through all of this he stood unharmed, but if she did not hurt him, certainly she angered him.

The imploring attitude he had seemed to adopt fell away and his massive body began to tremble in rage. One of the hands he held out to Armandra clenched and rose up threateningly, swept across to strike his own shoulder in a strangely human gesture of pride. The game was over, the 'offer' was withdrawn – now the Wind-Walker *demanded* obedience! He might as well have asked it of the wide seas of Earth or the desert's sands. She simply moved farther away and continued to rain down her lightnings, whose bolts became increasingly violent.

So much I saw before being drawn into the tide of renewed battle that washed across the roof. For with Armandra holding Ithaqua's attention so completely, his aerial invaders were on their own against the men of the plateau, and where the latter were concerned, no quarter would be asked and none given. Hearing my name on the lips of every man who fought for the plateau, I joined them, hurling myself headlong into the fighting.

It was then that Whitey found his way to me through the mass of struggling bodies. 'Hank,' he gasped, dragging me behind a natural wall of rock that protected one of the openings into the plateau. 'Hank, I have an idea.'

'A hunch?'

'No, just an idea. My hunch days are over.'

'All right, what is it?'

'Tracy has a star-stone with her, right? Well, if she can somehow manage to fasten it to a spearhead – tie it firmly with a thong or something – do you suppose you could land it on Ithaqua's warty hide?'

'He makes a big enough target,' I answered. 'I suppose I should be able to do it. Come on, let's see if we can get to Tracy and Jimmy.'

Making our way across the roof was not easy. Through gaps in the tumult we got occasional glimpses of the two of them, Jimmy fighting like a madman side by side with a massive Eskimo guardsman, and Tracy behind them, her back to the same rocky projection that had kept her safe from Ithaqua's ice-bomb, protecting their flanks with her star-stone. But halfway to them we got split up. The last I saw of Whitey for a while, he was tackling a lean Viking, while I myself was faced with a pair of hatchet-faced braves.

I was lucky, managing to kill both my men without being hurt. At the same time I discovered a strange thing: though there was more than one occasion when nearby guardsmen might have stepped in and made things easier, not one of them lifted a hand to help me. I had obviously reached new heights of legend; Sil-ber-hut-te could look after himself and wouldn't thank anyone for interfering!

But if I could look after myself, the same could no longer be said of Armandra. As I cleared a path for myself through the crush of fighting men, I saw that Armandra was almost spent. The energies she drew from the whirling clouds were less powerful, her stance less steady above the plateau's rim. And her father was beginning to enjoy his invulnerability. As the lightning rained about him, so he would use his great hands to deflect the bolts into the groups of furiously fighting men on the roof. It seemed of absolutely no concern to Ithaqua where these bolts fell or what mayhem they caused; the deaths of his own followers were of no consequence to him.

In any case, within the space of a few seconds more it could be seen that with or without Ithaqua's concern, his human allies were well and truly beaten. Though they fought a desperate, ragged retreat to the battlements, where at last the monstrous shadow of their lord and master fell upon them, still the men of the plateau followed them up, determined that not one of them would escape. The end came quickly even as I watched. Taking full advantage of their opportunity the plateau's soldiers made one last effort, forming an unbreakable wall and moving inexorably forward until the remaining kite-men were simply pushed off the roof into empty space. They fell in a screaming human rain from the rim.

Then I turned my eyes again to the sky, to the bloated figure of Ithaqua and the tiny shape of his daughter as their aerial confrontation continued. But that battle, too, if such an unequal contest could rightly be termed a battle, was almost done. Exhausted, Armandra seemed to waver in the sky, her eyes dulling and brightening spasmodically, while her father waxed ever more triumphant in his mockery of her efforts.

Now there was a complete absence of movement on the roof as every eye followed Armandra's struggle. I was on the point of reaching out to her with my mind to offer whatever mental assistance I could, when above the crazed howling of the wind and following immediately in the wake of yet another deflected bolt of lightning, I heard Whitey cry, 'Hank – I've got it!'

He was making his way to me across the death-strewn roof with Jimmy and Tracy on his heels. In his hand he carried his secret weapon, its fatal head held well out in front of and away from his body. And it was at that very moment that Ithaqua suddenly reached out and snatched Armandra out of the sky. Drained of all her strength, she made no effort to escape him but seemed simply to collapse, a doll in the fist of a giant.

'*Armandra, hang on!*' I cried out with my mind. She heard me, even though she was no longer strong enough to answer me, but what I had not reckoned with was that her father would also hear me. He did, and he must also have seen in my mind's eye a picture of the weapon I intended to use against him.

The Wind-Walker immediately turned to face me. He looked down upon me, and upon Whitey as he came rushing across the plateau's roof toward me. The monster's eyes slitted as they followed Whitey, then he lifted his free hand to the sky and thrust it into the lowering grey clouds.

'Whitey – look out!' I yelled, but my friend had also seen and knew what was going to happen. He *knew*, and on this occasion needed no precognition to tell him his fate.

Ithaqua moved closer, looming large over the roof as he hurled his ice-bomb. I saw it – saw Paul White's horrible but mercifully instant death beneath ten tons of ice that smashed down upon him like a meteorite – and I also saw his last heroic action in defiance of his destroyer. Not a second too soon, he slid the spear with its star-stone tip in my direction.

Skidding across the roof that weapon came, finally to slide to a halt at my feet. I stared at it for the merest moment, almost uncomprehendingly. Then, no longer fearing the stone sigil of Eld tied to the spear's blade – I was so numb with sick horror that I no longer felt or feared anything – snatched it up. And as I felt the unevenly balanced shaft in my hand, so the sickness and the horror went out of me, *driven* out by murderous hate and a lusting for red revenge!

I drew back my arm and aimed the spear at the Wind-Walker, who seemed suddenly to lose coordination. As I hurled the spear, he began to bring his hands up to guard his face.

What happened then, is not an easy thing to tell. It seemed to me that the spear moved through the air in a sort of slow motion, and that Ithaqua's hand moved even slower, so that when the weapon shot in through the flinching slit of his left eye I could easily trace the disappearance of its length into his head. Then things began to speed up again. The dull roar that had been growing in my ears burst into a howl of approval from the warriors on the roof; the sky seemed to bend downward; the back of Ithaqua's head flew open and a stream of molten gold flooded out, through the midst of which the spear with its star-stone sigil continued its curving flight out over the plateau's rim.

It had passed through him just like the tracers we fired at him from the plane's machine gun (how many centuries ago?) during our first encounter, but with much more devastating effect! For while bullets were of no consequence to Ithaqua, the seal of the Elder Gods was very different.

The Wind-Walker reeled like a man struck in the forehead with a hammer. For a second I thought he would topple out of the sky as he fought wildly to regain his balance. Then something fell from his hand as he lurched erratically to and fro. It was Armandra, spiralling down like an autumn leaf, the dull pinkish flush emanating from her more dully yet as she slowly sank, until at a height of about twenty feet the glow blinked out and she fell like a stone.

As I ran toward her still form I saw Ithaqua throw up his hands to his swollen, pulsating head. I saw him striking his temples with the flat of his hands in a mad frenzy, while the stream of golden sparks continued to issue from his left eye and the wound at the back of his head, and then I 'heard' a cry of what could only be described as purest alien anguish. It was his mental voice crying out against unbearable psychic stress, to which I automatically closed my mind lest I too feel his agony.

By the time I reached Armandra and knelt beside her, the Wind-Walker was lurching away down aerial paths, heading for the lonely sanctuary of his pyramid altar. But in contrast to his previous lordly stridings on the wings of the wind, now he moved with the spastic jerks and twitchings of a singed moth. He might well recover, but I knew that he would *never* forget.

4

The Last Transmission

(Recorded through the Medium of Juanita Alvarez)

And for the present, Juanita, there is little more to tell. I believe I have already told you that Armandra may be crippled. There seems to be some injury to her spine; Jimmy and Tracy, however – they at least are safe. Jimmy received a few cuts from the ice-bomb that killed poor brave Whitey, but nothing serious.

When we left the roof, Jimmy and Tracy went off together to mourn in private while I returned to Armandra's chambers. Of course, she was not there; she had been taken to be examined by the plateau's greatest doctors. I stood on the high balcony looking out over the white waste and waited for news. I stayed there, in what must have been a state of delayed shock, for five or six hours.

When Oontawa came to me in tears I thought at first that she brought terrible news, but that wasn't it. She only wanted me to go with her to where her man, Kota'na, was lying in one of the plateau's hospitals. They had only just found him near the gates of the central snow-ship keep. He had been brought in with a pitiful handful of wounded men. His injuries were severe but not fatal; he needed rest but would not submit either to the physician's wishes or their drugs until he had seen me. I went with her, hurrying down into the bowels of the plateau.

Kota'na, who had a small room of his own befitting his rank and status, was hanging onto consciousness waiting for me. When he saw me a grim, tired smile creased his handsome Indian features. His arms were caked with blood and he bore terrible scars on various parts of his body, but he was in no way about to die. It was as Oontawa had told me; rest and recuperation were all he required to bring him back to complete recovery.

Now Oontawa translated as I bent over Kota'na's bed.

'Lord Sil-ber-hut-te, I beg your forgiveness.'

'My forgiveness? For what, Kota'na? You fought for the plateau, for its princess, and for your woman, Oontawa. You fought well and commanded the bears and the men who handle them. You have no need to beg forgiveness of me.'

Then he lifted up his hand from where it hung unseen on the far side of his raised pallet. His fingers were clenched in hair that was full of clotted blood, black hair rooted in the roughly severed head of Northan, which hung from Kota'na's fist and stared at me with wide, glassy eyes.

'Forgive me, Lord, for I knew that you would want him for yourself – and knowing it, I killed him. I tried to take him alive, but he would not let me. Take his head, it belongs to you.'

'No.' I shook my head at his offer. 'The trophy is yours, Kota'na. Let it hang in your lodge so that your children will know of my debt to you, that their father killed Sil-ber-hut-te's great enemy, the traitor Northan. For this deed, I thank you.'

Five minutes later, after accepting a drugged drink, Kota'na fell asleep and the physicians were able to begin washing him and cleaning his wounds. But it took them as long again to pry open his hand and remove Northan's head.

As for Ithaqua; he too appears to be resting. The monster crouches atop his pyramid altar and cradles his head in his hands. His left eye is half closed – yellow sparks

221

drip from it like pus – and a dark spot is visible at the back of his head. Since his wounds were not fatal, I can only assume that he is recuperating. He has shrunk down into himself somewhat, though his size is still four or five times greater than that of a man. Even now I can see him as I gaze out across the white waste through my binoculars, and –

What was that?

Strange, I thought for a moment that –

But no, I must have been mistaken. Did you feel anything, Juanita? It seemed as though someone were listening in on our conversation. You didn't? Good. And yet I could have sworn that just for a moment I saw Ithaqua turn his head to peer evilly at the plateau out of his good eye . . .

A messenger has just arrived, sent by the physicians who attend Armandra. He seems to be quite delighted but I can't understand a word he says. It appears I am to accompany him.

I'll contact you again as soon as I have news.

NOTE:
The time was 5:50 P.M. on June 6 when Juanita Alvarez recorded that last hopeful message from Hank Silberhutte. His telepathic vibrations were then absent for some two hours, until, at 7:45 P.M., Juanita made the following, final, brief contact with him.

'Juanita, I'm back.

'*Everything is going to be all right!* I'm back on the balcony now, but I've just finished tidying up Armandra's – no, *our* – chambers, getting the place ready for her. She's conscious and they're carrying her up here right now. She's going to be fine, but she'll need a lot of rest and quiet. All she wanted when she awakened was to be with me. God, Juanita, but you must be able to *feel* how happy I am! It's as if a terrible black cloud were suddenly lif –

'*Again!* And this time there can be no doubt about it. I was watching Ithaqua through the glasses while I talked to you. It was him, listening in, and suddenly he turned and looked at me – and he smiled in a terrible way!

'Juanita, I think he saw right through me – *to you!*

'But what in the . . . this? There seems . . . sort . . . interference. It's *him*! Ithaqua is scrambling my . . . losing you! And now . . . the altar and limping off across the sky. He looks back at me and . . . hideous laughter! . . . revenge? My God, it's you, Juanita. He can no longer hurt us *so he's coming for you!*

'Tell Peaslee he has to look after you. Tell him –'

FINAL NOTE: For three long months, into the middle of September, Juanita stayed at Miskatonic and spent every minute of every day trying to reestablish contact with Hank. She never heard from him again, and having turned down my offer to take up a position with the Wilmarth Foundation, she left Arkham in the third week of the month.

When she went she took with her one of the star-stones of ancient Mnar, a genuine stone found with others by our African expeditions in 1959. We kept in contact until early the next year. When last I heard from her she was making wedding arrangements in Monterrey.

In March of the new year I learned how, along with her husband, she was killed in an automobile accident near Regina, Canada, where they were honeymooning. The car had been blown off the road and down a sheer drop in a 'freak storm'. I made inquiries and discovered that they had been returning to their hotel after a show. The gown Juanita was wearing had a plunging neckline – not the kind of gown she could wear her star-stone with.

As for Hank Silberhutte, his sister Tracy, and James Graywing Franklin: so far as I am aware they are still on

Borea, a world at the edge of strange dimensions, some-where out in remote regions of space and time.

My telepathic team at Miskatonic still occasionally try, without reward to date, to reestablish contact with Hank, and I personally will never give up hope.

– Wingate Peaslee.